MARTHA MOORE

Delacorte Press

Published by
Delacorte Press
Bantam Doubleday Dell Publishing Group, Inc.
1540 Broadway • New York, New York 10036

Library of Congress Cataloging-in-Publication Data
Moore, Martha.
Under the mermaid angel / Martha Moore.
p. cm.
Summary: Through an unusual friendship with her thirty-year-old neighbor in a Texas trailer park, thirteen-year-old Jesse learns that what's inside a person is more important than what's outside.
ISBN 0-385-32160-0
[1. Friendship—Fiction. 2. Schools—Fiction. 3. Texas—Fiction. 4. Brothers and sisters—Fiction.] I. Title.
PZ7.M78715Un 1995
[Fic]—dc20 95-1991
CIP
AC

The text of this book is set in 12-point Goudy Old Style.
Book design by Vikki Sheatsley
Manufactured in the United States of America
October 1995
10 9 8 7 6 5 4 3 2 1

For Howard, Peter and Michael
and in memory of my mother,
Peggy Goodman

CHAPTER 1

Six springtimes have passed since William III left us. I mean died. Mama said it wasn't anybody's fault, it was just one of those things. Right after it happened, though, she put all his toys in a plastic sack and set them out on the porch for the Salvation Army truck, like it really was someone's fault. I asked her why she gave them away so soon—the little monkey that played cymbals, the rubber elephant that squeaked, everything—and she just said it was time. But she was crying like it really wasn't time at all.

A few months later Daddy called the White House and got an eight-by-ten picture of the President sitting on his horse, signed near the horse's back legs. Mama framed it and put it on the wall over the TV set for good luck.

The next spring she had another baby, and that was Doris Ray. After her came the twins, Jimmy and Roy Dean. Pretty soon, William III got completely erased from our lives and it was almost like he had never even lived at all.

The only thing was I couldn't forget that easy. Because the truth, the thing I could never tell anybody, is that William III didn't die all at once. He died in parts, every night at supper.

What I mean is this: For weeks while he was sick Mama always said the same thing, "Pray for William III, Jesse." Every night, I shook my head.

"Pray he gets well before the iris bloom," she'd beg. But I wouldn't say the magic words that might've changed God's mind. I sat quiet and let my brother die.

For all these years, I never told anybody, not even a best friend, which was something I didn't have anyway. But all that changed when Roxanne moved into the trailer next door.

Mama didn't like her much. She said Roxanne was anything but respectable. For one thing, it was okay with me that Roxanne had a Liberty Bell tattooed on her chest. It wasn't okay with Mama. Another thing was, Mama said Roxanne was too old to be my friend. I disagreed.

I think if you're thirteen, you're old enough to choose your friends. Roxanne used to say friendship's measured by heart-time, not clock-time, and I know that's true because with Roxanne the years didn't make any difference at all. Even though she was thirty, almost thirty-one, she was my very best friend.

I met Roxanne the day after Christmas. Mama was making us take down the decorations, which is just one reason I hate the holidays. Christmas, to me, is a lot of work followed by the most boring week of the year before school starts up again.

After William III left, I could see things really clear. For example the skates. That year I'd wanted white shoe skates with blue pom-poms on the toes. But when I found them under the tree, all I could see were the big creases in the leather covered with chalky white shoe polish.

"Mrs. Santa tried them out first," Mama tried to explain. "She wanted to make sure they worked real good."

All my past Christmas dolls with their slick faces and homemade clothes lit up in my mind like a string of lights. I knew Mama shopped at the thrift store, but until then I never guessed Christmas came from there, too.

This year seemed like it wasn't going to be any different from the rest. Then I heard a knock at the door.

"Somebody's here," Doris Ray yelled, pulling at my sweatpants. I was standing on the recliner trying to undo the last ornament, the angel at the very top of the tree.

Mama hollered from the bedroom, "Get the door, Jesse."

"Get the door," Doris Ray echoed.

"Okay, okay," I said, reaching for the treetop one last time. I grabbed the angel's foot and yanked. The whole tree fell to the floor.

"Now look what you did," I said to my sister. I picked up the angel and twirled it by the hair. It looked all right.

By then Doris Ray and the boys were lined up at the window looking out. I stopped and peeked, too. Roxanne was standing there wearing a huge black furry coat and these big cat-eye sunglasses covered in green rhinestones. Her long red hair flared out like a fire alarm. I recognized her right away as our new neighbor.

"You want to come in?" I asked, opening the screen door a crack.

"Sure," she said and stepped inside, not even mentioning the upside-down Christmas tree. "Y'all have any jumper cables? My car won't start and I was supposed to've been at work thirty minutes ago. By the way, my name's Roxanne, what's yours?"

I said it was Jesse and that I thought we had some jumper cables in a grocery sack in the pantry. I realized I was still holding that dumb plastic angel, but before I could set it down, she took my chin in her hand and looked into my eyes. "You have the most beautiful eyes I have ever seen," she said. "They're like moon pools. Deep green moon pools. With flecks of gold."

I didn't know what to do, so when she let go I said, "We learned in science that there isn't any water on the moon, and if there was a pool, it probably wouldn't be green because you wouldn't have photosynthesis."

Roxanne grinned. She said that might be perfectly true in a scientific sense, but in a more important sense, green moon pools definitely existed.

"What do you see when you look at the moon, Jesse?"

"I don't know," I said, picking at the star behind the angel where all the fake gold was peeling off. "Craters, shadows, I guess."

"Well, I see a mother holding a baby," Roxanne said. "The moon pools are the mother's eyes."

She seemed pretty sure about things so after she got the jumper cables and left, I looked in the bathroom mirror for at least five minutes. I didn't see anything except plain green eyes with a few mustard dots. No moon pools. No gold. And that night the moon looked the same as ever. But from that time on, I knew Roxanne was different from anyone I had ever known in Ida, Texas. And for some crazy reason we got to be friends, even though two people couldn't be more different from each other.

For one thing, Roxanne wore nothing but push-up bras. She said that what a girl wears underneath determines how she feels about herself. She might've been joking, but I believed her because all my panties were white cotton from a mail-order catalog, and I felt rotten about myself.

Take my hair for instance. Roxanne's hung to her waist like a mermaid's and the color was dark red brick, the kind Mama wants for a house someday. Mine, on the other hand, is straight and thin and the color of dirt when it hasn't rained in a long time. Nobody would want a house that color. Mama says my hair is exactly like her aunt Willa's, fine as a duck's behind.

She says Willa's was so stringy and flyaway she finally pinned it into a little flat knot on top of her head, had to use about fifty bobby pins, and wore a knit cap pulled down over it.

Mama's telling the truth, I know, because I saw a picture of Willa in an old family album. She sat in a porch swing scowling and wearing that knit cap pulled down to her ears.

Plus, I'm flat-chested. Roxanne loaned me her $13.95 breast developer, but having any room to myself for twenty minutes a day is a near impossibility where I live.

First there's my kid sister, Doris Ray. Sharing a room with a five-year-old is no picnic, let me tell you. I hardly get a minute's peace. "Jesse, can I have a banana?" "Jesse, me and Mark got engaged today." "Jesse, I wish I was a dolphin." Lord, I wish I was anything, anywhere but in a double bed with a five-year-old.

And then there's the twin boys. Just getting them bathed at night is major. They scream and holler. Think they're going down the drain with the bathwater. It's crazy, I think. When you're little, you can't figure out who you are on the outside, then when you get older you don't know who you are on the inside. Roxanne said when you finally start figuring it all out, it doesn't even matter anymore.

Being around her made me feel as light as a balloon, and I hoped she'd never leave. But from the very first, Roxanne said she wanted to go to Florida, get a job on a love boat. I hoped that'd be a long time off because when people move out of the trailer court, they almost never come back.

Her leaving would mean no more walks to the bait store for moon pies and ginger ale. No more long talks.

And all those times she'd lay her face on the ironing board and I'd stretch out that long red hair to the end and iron it so pretty and smooth. All those times would be gone. When you have a best friend, the first one in a long, long time, you never want it to end.

CHAPTER 2

I wondered why someone like Roxanne would come to Ida. Besides the plastics factory where Daddy works, there's not much here. We have a few churches, a Laundromat, a drugstore that's also the bus station, Murphy's department store, a feed store, two grocery stores and a few other things, but you have to drive twenty miles just to get to a decent movie theater. Except for Mr. Arthur's Wax Museum, there's not much that's fun to do.

People say the only reason to move to Ida is to hide from something. That's what I figured about Roxanne. Why else would she move to just about the most boring place in the universe? New Year's Day we were sitting on the floor in her living room painting Flaming Tomato polish on our toenails when I asked her.

"For meteor showers," she said. "The sky in these parts is so clear. In the city you can sit out all night and never see one falling star." She put the brush back into the bottle and stretched out her long legs, spreading her toes so the polish wouldn't get messed up. "Tonight's a big one. In Ida it'll be easier to see."

I could tell she didn't want to say why she really came. "So you came all the way to Ida to work part-time at a truck stop and watch the stars?"

"And make wishes," she said. "Without falling stars, how would your wishes come true?" She stood up and looked at me like she really expected an answer.

When I didn't say anything, she said, "I've got to get ready for work. Ask your mother if you can come over when I get off and sleep out."

I knew Mama wouldn't like the idea. She wouldn't want me hanging around Roxanne for a whole night.

"I'm not real crazy about that Roxanne," she said later when I asked her. She was rolling out dough for biscuits and she pressed the rolling pin down real hard, stretching the dough out a lot thinner than it should have been.

"Mama, it'll help in science. Plus, you told Daddy that Roxanne's the best neighbor we've had in a long time," I told her.

"Jesse," she said, dumping the flour out hard enough to make a cloud in front of her face, "I said I was glad she picked up all that old scrap metal from the front yard when she moved in. The place looks a good bit neater than I've seen it in a while. But as a friend for you, I don't know."

"You just don't like it that she has a tattoo," I said, watching her stamp circles into the dough.

A couple of days after Roxanne came over to borrow the jumper cables, Mama and I were out back hanging clothes on the line. It was a warm day and Roxanne walked over wearing tight blue jeans and a sequined T-shirt that was cut real low in front.

"Can you believe this weather?" she'd said. "That's what I like about this part of the country, it's so unpredictable." When she bent over to pick up a wet sock out of the basket to help, she caught Mama staring right at her tattoo.

"Y'all looking at my Liberty Bell?" she asked.

Mama's face got red and she said something about how she was just looking for another pair of Daddy's undershorts.

"It's okay," Roxanne said. "I got it right after my divorce was final." She pulled the top of her T-shirt down farther and pointed to a line on the bell. "Used to say Robert, but I got the name changed into a crack. You know," she said, grinning, "the crack in the Liberty Bell?"

Mama had clamped her teeth together just like she was doing now as she rolled out some more dough.

"You don't like it she's divorced?" I wasn't going to give up. "What about Aunt June? She got a divorce and you like her, don't you?" Aunt June is Mama's younger sister and Mama doesn't like anybody saying anything bad about her.

"I haven't gotten to do one fun thing over the holidays, and they're just about over," I added. "And we'll just be a few feet away from your bedroom window. Please?"

"Jess-see," she said slowly, her voice sounding like a balloon that was losing air fast. "All right, you can go, but you have to take Doris Ray. And plenty of blankets," she added.

Doris Ray stood at the kitchen table beating a little wad of dough with her fist. She had flour in her hair and on her face and she looked at me real smart-like, and started singing, "I get to sleep outside . . . I get to sleep outside . . . with Jesse," she added for extra emphasis just to annoy me.

"And I'm gonna bring a star cup," she sang out. "I'm gonna catch me a whole cup of stars!"

I told her she wouldn't be doing that because she'd have to go to sleep before the stars even happened, but she said she was going to stay awake as long as I did.

"It's not anything but a bunch of dumb falling stars," I told her.

"I might catch one if I stay awake," she whined, twisting the curl at her ear like she always does.

"Your hair is going to fall out if you keep doing that," I nagged. "Besides, if you're outside with us, a meteor could crash down on you while you're running around trying to catch things."

"You're teasing," she said. You can't scare Doris Ray from doing anything. I knew she'd stay awake for the whole meteor shower if it killed her.

Late that night after Roxanne got in from work, Doris Ray and I dragged a mattress into the backyard. Roxanne brought her beanbag chair to sleep on and she said she was glad Doris Ray could come.

"It is one beautiful night," she said, twirling around in

her fake fur. She called the coat her "moo-ton," which sounded like a kind of Chinese food to me. Underneath she was still wearing her pink waitress dress and matching pink tennis shoes and she spread her arms out like a ballerina.

"Come on, Doris Ray, let's do a pirouette." She lifted Doris Ray and helped her stand on her toes, then twirled her around. They were giggling and carrying on and I figured someone would be out there hollering at us to get quiet pretty soon.

No one came, though, and Roxanne went in to change clothes. When she came out she looked like she was dressed for a party instead of sleeping out. She was wearing some crazy leopard-spotted leotards and a gold sparkly blouse, and, of course, that big coat of hers. She threw a paper sack toward Doris Ray, who was sitting on the ground wrapped in a blanket.

"Here, honey. It's confetti for when the stars come pouring down." Doris Ray jumped up and down acting real stupid. I couldn't believe she'd get so excited over a little bag of cut up comics from the Sunday paper.

Finally, she settled down and we all sat in the dark waiting for something to happen.

"Is that the warmest coat you have?" Roxanne asked me, looking at my thin jacket.

"It'll do," I said, and I pulled it tighter around me. I was thinking it sure wasn't cold enough for the rug she wore.

"Y'all have your wishes thought up?" Roxanne changed the subject.

"I do. I do," Doris Ray shrieked. "I'm gonna wish that—"

"Don't tell, baby," Roxanne interrupted. "It's gotta be a secret."

"Oh," Doris Ray whispered.

"You got some wishes planned, Jesse? You can make as many as you want tonight," Roxanne said.

"Nope. Not me. I don't believe in that stuff. I just want to see the stars. That's enough. We've read about these things in science."

Roxanne said, "Well, I've got only one wish. And I'm going to use it for every star that falls. It'll have to come true."

"Are all the stars going to fall down?" Doris Ray asked. She can ask the dumbest questions.

"No, sweetheart," Roxanne answered. "There'll still be millions and millions of them. When one falls down, it leaves seeds behind for about a dozen more." I figured I'd have to get Doris Ray straightened out later, but I let Roxanne go on about her crazy ideas.

"Someone once said that when falling stars hit the ocean, they harden and become starfish," she added.

Doris Ray moved over to Roxanne's chair and Roxanne put her arm around her. "Just watch, sweetie pie, you'll see."

It was real early in the morning when Roxanne woke us up, me on the mattress and Doris Ray on her lap.

"Did we miss it?" I asked.

"No, look," she said. "Open your eyes."

When I did, the first thing I noticed was the quiet. It was like the whole trailer park had moved inside another world, one without any sound. I felt like I was inside one of those glass balls that you shake and watch the snow fall down, except the snowflakes were stars. Dozens, maybe hundreds, poured down on us. I forgot all about Doris Ray and Roxanne and everything else. It was just me and the stars, a thousand sparkly white threads pushing out of the night, and each one shooting straight at me.

Finally, I felt Doris Ray breathing beside me. She can't stand to be still for very long. Giggling, she hopped up and grabbed Roxanne's sack of confetti.

"Shhh" Roxanne said, putting her finger to her mouth. "Be real quiet so the magic can happen." Doris Ray pressed her lips together and, without a sound, skipped around the yard tossing fistfuls of confetti into the air.

Roxanne couldn't stand it. She laughed and got a handful, too, and pretty soon I was covered in the stuff, but I stayed on my back on the ground and didn't even care.

"Make a wish, make a hundred wishes," Roxanne said, stretching her arms up to the sky. Doris Ray picked up her cup and held it as high as she could.

"Come on, star, just one, fall into my cup," she whispered to the air.

I sat up. "I read that a star is about a million miles in diameter, about the size of the sun. They just look little because they're so far away," I said.

"A star wouldn't fit in a cup, then, would it?" Doris Ray said, setting her cup in the dirt by the clothesline.

Roxanne answered. "No, sugar, not a whole star, but you might catch some stardust."

"Well, not exactly," I told both of them. "Meteor showers usually come from comets. The comet comes around our part of the earth every so often and when it does, it leaves a trail of stuff, kind of like what you see floating around in the light that comes through the window. It's pretty and all, but it's just that floaty stuff we're seeing, not stars."

"Is she right?" Doris Ray asked Roxanne.

Before she had a chance to answer, I added, "So there's no such thing as stardust, at least not the kind you could catch."

Roxanne lay down on the ground with her hands under her head. "Well, maybe stardust is invisible. But I think when it lands on people it makes their hearts sparkle, and their eyes and voices, too."

"We saw a picture at school of a gigantic hole left by a meteor," I said. "Sometimes meteorites don't vaporize and come crashing to earth."

Doris Ray had turned on the flashlight and was examining the inside of her empty cup. I saw her lip tremble in the light.

"Jesse, do you *really* think one will come crashing down here?" She held her light to the sky and searched. I figured I could get her to crying if I wanted to.

"No, that won't happen," I said.

"I love you, Jesse," Doris Ray's voice sounded small and sweet like a tiny Christmas bell.

"Yeah," I said. "I love you too, kid."

"Just think," Roxanne said, still lying on her back and

gazing at the sky. "Those words will float in space forever. I heard that everything you say your whole life is floating around in space."

I doubted Roxanne was right, but if she was, I wondered if Mama's words telling me to pray for William III were out there. My half-finished prayer would be limping through space after them, with the part about William III missing forever and ever.

Finally, the meteor shower slowed to only one or two streaks and the wind picked up, making eerie flapping noises in the trees. When I was Doris Ray's age and heard that sound at night, I thought some birds had their wings caught in the branches and couldn't get away. It scared me real bad. Past the row of poplars way over the fence, somebody's cats were fighting. I told Roxanne and my sister good night and closed my eyes and went to sleep.

CHAPTER 3

Doris Ray, Roxanne and I slept right through the sunrise the next morning. We might've slept until noon, but it was Sunday and Mama sent Daddy to wake us up for church.

"Jesse! Jesse!" My name sounded far away. I opened one eye and saw Daddy standing several feet from us, next to Roxanne's crape myrtle. He wore his gray sweatpants and Leonard's Feed Store T-shirt and was waving at me with a red baseball cap.

I was lying on the mattress, and Roxanne and Doris Ray were in a big furry lump curled up on the beanbag chair.

"Get up, Jesse," Daddy whispered in a gravelly voice. "Get Doris Ray and y'all get on home."

I stood up and looked around. Our confetti had

turned to smelly clumps, and some dried-up leaves had blown into Doris Ray's star cup.

I nudged Doris Ray's shoulder and she opened her eyes, squinting up at the sky. "Are the stars all gone?" she asked.

"Yep," I whispered. "Daddy said we have to get up. Gotta get ready for church. Don't wake up Roxanne."

Doris Ray uncurled herself from the chair and stretched while Roxanne slept on as peaceful as ever. We tiptoed across the yard toward our trailer. I looked over at Doris Ray. Her face was dirty and the electricity from sleeping on a plastic chair made her hair stand out from her head like a halo.

"You're a mess," I said. She scrunched her nose and grinned.

"We had fun, didn't we, Jesse?"

"Yeah," I said. "We sure did."

We got to church late and it was a disaster, mostly because I had to sit next to Frankenstein. His real name is Franklin Harris, and he's the biggest jerk in the eighth grade. He's taller than most of the guys and kind of skinny. But it's not the way he looks, which is pretty normal for a guy, I guess. The problem is the way he acts.

For example at church: The first song we sang was "He Leadeth Me." Frankenstein poked me in the ribs with his elbow, then pointed to something he'd scribbled on his bulletin. I looked real close and he'd written, "Under the Sheets." I didn't know what he was talking about and I shook my head. Pretty soon he poked me again. "He Leadeth Me . . . Under the Sheets."

I looked over at his parents, Dr. Harris and Mrs. Harris. Their eyes were glued to the front. Frankenstein's parents are too nice for their son. Dr. Harris runs the clinic downtown. Mrs. Harris is an artist and also raises exotic flowers. She has a greenhouse in her very own backyard where she grows all kinds of plants, some of them from as far away as Japan. One day Frankenstein bragged in the school cafeteria that he'd sneaked in there at night and pulled out every bird-of-paradise by the roots. He said he'd made little nooses out of pipe cleaners and had hung the flowers in the doorway.

I believed him because, like I said, he's a real jerk. During Pastor Cordell's announcements, Frankenstein flipped through the hymnal pointing to song titles: "Softly and Tenderly . . . Under the Sheets," "Holy, Holy, Holy . . . Under the Sheets" and "Great Is Thy Faithfulness . . . Under the Sheets."

I scooted away from him as far as I could until we had to stand for the prayer. My eyes were closed and I was thinking about the meteor shower, feeling real calm and peaceful like you're supposed to feel at church. The prayer finally ended and I sat down—or tried to anyway.

During the prayer, Frankenstein had piled a stack of hymnbooks underneath me. When I tried to sit down I smacked right into them. The books went flying out and I slid down and hit my tailbone on the edge of the pew. Mama said I could have fallen without the scream. But I said it wasn't a scream, just a little yelp, and it could have been a whole lot more. I told Roxanne all about it after lunch.

"Look, Jesse," she said, "forget it. He's probably battling testosterone."

"I can't believe you're defending him!" I said. "I don't think he's battling tes . . . whatever you call it or anything else. I hate him!"

"Tell you what," Roxanne answered. "Let's do something fun."

"You're in Ida, remember?" I said with as much sarcasm as I could.

"I want to go to the wax museum. Go ask your mother and I'll meet you outside after I get my eyelashes on."

It's beyond me why you have to wear false eyelashes to go to downtown Ida, but I didn't say anything. Pretty soon we were on our way to Mr. Alexander Arthur's Famous Wax Museum.

CHAPTER 4

Mr. Arthur's wax museum used to be an old church that was empty for a lot of years. But when Mr. Arthur bought it, his family moved into a few rooms on the ground floor and the basement became the museum. The main attraction, the one he advertises on his sign outside, is the wax replica of the Last Supper. He's only got Jesus and five disciples, though, and they're in pretty bad shape.

Peter is missing an eye, which Mr. Arthur covered with a pirate's patch. And Matthew's got a finger broken off. Thomas and Judas were pretty worn out when Mr. Arthur bought them, and John's left ear got too close to a fire. But Jesus is still in pretty good condition.

In fact, most of the people in town have had their picture taken alongside him at one time or another. Daddy says, though, that everybody would know it wasn't real because Jesus' lips are too red and the wall behind the exhibit has too many nail holes and too much paint peeled off. Mama says having your picture made with Jesus is plain low class.

I hadn't seen Mr. Arthur since just after Thanksgiving when his wife, Ruby, died. It had snowed, which it hardly ever does around here, and Mama and I had taken over a pot of chili. That day he looked a mess. The bow tie he always wore hung lopsided at his neck and half his shirttail stuck out. I whispered to Mama that he had on two different kinds of shoes, one black and one tan. He needed to shave and his hair spread out in little white sprigs all over his head. Mama said he just needed a woman to take care of him.

After the funeral, people talked about seeing Mr. Arthur squatting in front of his house planting the flowers from all the funeral sprays. Someone told him that you can't plant flowers that have already been cut, but he kept digging holes through the leftover snow and sticking in a carnation or a mum and pressing the icy mud around it to hold it up. The next morning when Daddy drove us into town to church, all the flowers had frozen like Popsicles in a circle around his house. When I told Roxanne about it she said he just has his quirks. Everybody's got some, she said.

You might say one of Mr. Arthur's quirks is what he did with Judas. At one time Judas sat at the table with the other disciples, but people in town raised such a ruckus that Mr. Arthur put an umpire's uniform on him and moved him away from the Lord's table into the baseball section.

Baseball was the love of Mr. Arthur's life. He used to tell me, "Jesse, there's magic in baseball. Put on a uniform and you're changed. You're a better person for it." Baseball is something Mr. Arthur definitely believed in. But that was before he came down sick.

Some people say he hadn't been in his right mind for years and that he took a downhill plunge when Ruby died. Until recently, though, I thought Mr. Arthur was perfectly fine. He was different, but that's why I liked him. Just walking into his museum made me feel like I was somewhere else besides Ida, Texas.

First of all, when people come into the wax museum they're greeted by Queen Elizabeth I, who's standing with one foot propped on a globe of the world. She's got orange hair piled tall in a stack on her head and blue eyes that follow you. In one hand she's holding a toy ship to represent her defeat of the Spanish Armada, and in her other hand she's got a baton that belonged to Raquel Henson, head twirler the year our football team went to State.

Mr. Arthur never could afford real queen's clothes, so he dressed her in his daughter's old purple taffeta prom dress and silver shoes. He added sparkle wherever he could—rings on every finger, five bracelets on one arm, and a rhinestone crown. She looked rich and powerful and that was the main point.

Mr. Arthur used to say to me, "Jesse, you're a young woman. Like Queen Elizabeth here, the world is at your feet." I thought about Mama standing at the ironing board for hours at a time. And Daddy forever asking her to bring him stuff—iced tea, gingerbread, anything he could think of. If the world was at Mama's feet, she'd have to vacuum it.

Besides wax, Mr. Arthur also has the strangest cap collection ever. These are not your typical caps—not like Daddy's stamped with Ed's Plumbing or Joe's Hot Rod House. Most of them aren't real caps at all. They're just shapes of caps cut from different colors of construction paper. Mr. Arthur drew a tiny baseball team logo on each one and pasted each cap onto one of the hundreds of photos that hang in the hallway of the museum. For example, Abraham Lincoln is wearing a Cardinals cap and George Washington a Royals. Last year when I brought in my school picture, Mr. Arthur asked, "What team you want to be on, Jesse, Red Sox, Yankees, Rangers, Giants? You name it, pick a winner, Jess." I picked the Orioles because they're a bird and I've never seen one of those kind, so Mr. Arthur made a little black-and-orange cap and pasted it on my picture. Back then he'd been working on the 1948 Arthur family reunion picture.

"Jess, my girl, I've got to make forty-seven caps for this one," he said. "Eight of 'em's babies—those extra-small ones are doozies." I asked if he couldn't just skip the babies. No one would expect them to have hats.

"Nope," he said. "Them little 'uns, four of them went on to fight in the Vietnam War. Two of them died over there." In Mr. Arthur's opinion, the babies needed hats more than anybody. Also he said he couldn't decide whether to give each person a different team or sort it out by families.

"What do you think, Jesse?" He was so serious when

he asked the question, twirling his white mustache and biting his bottom lip. It made me feel like I wanted to help him, like picking the right teams made a difference somehow.

"You could make the little ones who'll go off to fight the war a special group," I said.

"That's it!" Mr. Arthur said. "They'll be the Brooklyn Dodgers." He told me that team always had real bad luck. "You're just brilliant, Jess, my girl," he said. "I think you'll be my partner in the cap business!"

I thought about that statement as Roxanne and I came in the door of the museum. I looked around to see if he had finished the reunion picture. It was half done, and a few other pictures hung completely empty of caps. I didn't see Mr. Arthur anywhere.

Elma Faye Arthur, Mr. Arthur's daughter, was working up front when we arrived. She took our twenty-five cents each to get in, and told us the museum would probably close in the spring.

"Daddy's got Alzheimer's," she said, pronouncing it like "All-timers," which I know is wrong because we had learned about it in health class. "Course we can't know for sure until he dies and the doctor can get a little scrap of his brain to look at, but he's got it." She popped her gum and slapped at a fly that landed on her arm.

Elma is downright crude, as Mama would say. I say she belongs in the fairy tale with the ice witch. One of these days she'll be talking on and on and she'll just start freezing in place until she's a giant ice cube.

She went on to tell us that the doctor said her daddy's "men-tile" disease, which she pronounced like it was some kind of floor covering, was starting to advance past the early stages. She popped her gum again and put her hands on her big hips.

"Daddy's in there now with more of them idiotic pictures of his. He's got it in his little head that he has to make a hat for every damn picture left on the wall. As soon as he gets out the scissors and paper, though, he can't even remember what they're for." She narrowed her eyes so that her eye shadow clumped in the wrinkles of her eyelids like little blue clouds.

"One thing's for sure," she told us, "he's not taking that stuff to Purple Paradise. They allow five pictures, that's all. Besides, Daddy won't be allowed to have his own scissors."

Mr. Arthur shuffled into the room and Elma changed the tone of her voice to kind of how some people talk to poodles.

"Here's my daddy-kins," she cooed. "Daddy-kins will have a whole craft hour every day to make all sorts of useful things." Elma carried on about some of the fancy projects she'd seen at the home. The prettiest was an old high-heeled shoe they'd covered in macaroni and sprayed gold.

"It's the cutest little ivy planter you've ever laid your eyes on," she told us. There was a coin bank shaped like a dog with long black ears, too. "Can y'all believe they made that thing out of a two-liter Coke bottle?" Elma carried on and on about pot holders and bean pictures and toilet-paper covers and a lot of other dumb projects.

You'd think she wanted to live in Purple Paradise herself she got so excited, waving her hands around and all.

Her daddy just stood there looking at her like he wasn't even hearing what she was saying.

It did seem that Mr. Arthur had changed a whole lot in the weeks since I'd seen him last. He didn't even say hi to me and when I introduced Roxanne, his eyes darted around the room like a sparrow caught in an attic. Then he stared at me and grinned. "You're some—body," he drawled. "Ibbitty, dibbitty, doobitty—ain't she sweet just a-walking down the street?"

"It's me, Mr. Arthur. Jesse. Jess." I looked into his eyes.

Elma said, "Oh, Daddy knows you. He just can't think of your name. He don't even know mine half the time. And why he says those silly words from old songs, I don't know. This morning he wandered off and the sheriff brought him back. Said he was digging through trash cans." Mr. Arthur rocked back and forth on his heels.

I glanced at Roxanne. She looked worried. "Come on, Jesse, let's go look around."

We went to the Last Supper display, which was in a dark corner of the basement. Mr. Arthur put it there not because it wasn't important, but because he wanted it to be authentic.

"The disciples didn't eat in any lit-up restaurant," he'd told me one time. "They had to hide on account of the fact that people didn't understand. People hate what they can't understand."

What he said was true because a couple of years ago people got mad when he bought Ruby an angel for her birthday. He'd hung it on wires over the Lord's table, but the part people didn't like was that it wasn't a regular angel. It was a mermaid with wings, which didn't fit the Bible anywhere.

"I never saw any angels with fish tails," I'd told him.

"How many angels have you seen, Jess?" he had asked me.

I said not any up close, but I'd seen enough pictures to know they didn't have scales or tails, either.

"Mermaids, my dear, are underwater angels, didn't you know that?" he'd asked. "I'm making the invisible visible." I figured no one could argue with that, even though some people refused to visit the museum anymore.

Roxanne really liked the mermaid angel, especially after I'd told her what Mr. Arthur said about the invisible. "It's like that wax Jesus," she said. "It's not the real thing, it's just supposed to remind us of the real thing. Truth isn't something you can see straight out."

I said I had a hard enough time understanding what I could see straight out without worrying about what I couldn't see.

We stood looking at the angel for a while, then Roxanne grabbed me by the hand and pulled me away from the Lord's table to Mr. Arthur's animal exhibit where he kept a lot of odd things, like his two-headed chicken and the bird born with only one wing.

"Jesse, what's the one thing Mr. Arthur hasn't finished?" Roxanne said as she stroked the fur on a cat that a taxidermist had stuffed.

"I guess his cap collection," I said.

"Well, we've got to help him with it. He'll never get it done by himself."

"But Elma isn't going to let him take it, anyway."

"That's not the point, Jesse," she said. "It's his work and he needs to see it done. We're going to help him."

I knew Roxanne was determined.

"Jesse," she said, "didn't you ever wish you could finish an impossible job? Just once?"

I thought. "When I was little," I said, "I used to sweep the dirt out in front of our trailer hoping I'd find gold. And I spent almost a whole summer trying to dig a hole to China. Now I know better."

"Well, knowing better doesn't always make us happy, does it?" Roxanne said. "Maybe Mr. Arthur does have Alzheimer's. If he does, he won't get better. Only worse. He'll forget all about his caps. He might forget how to eat or go to the bathroom."

"Do you think he'll die?" I couldn't imagine Mr. Arthur being gone forever.

"Probably. At least eventually. But with Alzheimer's it's not dying that's so bad, it's living. We're going to help him finish those caps. It's important."

When Roxanne's got a plan, nothing can stop her.

CHAPTER 5

When school started back up after the holidays, things got busy. Roxanne worked most weekends and it was almost Valentine's Day before she talked about going back to Mr. Arthur's to make the caps.

"I think it'd be a good way to celebrate," she said as we sat on the floor in her kitchen, taking a break from counting rice. Roxanne was determined to win a trip for two to New Orleans and all you had to do was count the grains in a five-pound bag of rice.

"Celebrate what?" I asked, pushing the rice I'd counted into a pile.

"Valentine's," she said, acting real surprised. "Don't you usually do something?"

"Nope," I answered. "Not since the third grade when we decorated mailboxes."

"Well, I think it'd be a good day to finish Mr. Arthur's caps," she said, resting her cheek on her hand.

"Does that mean we can forget about counting the rest of this stupid rice?" I asked.

"Don't you want to go to New Orleans with me?"

"You and I both know there's some kind of gimmick. We'd be lucky to win a free trip to downtown Ida. It'd take us a lifetime to count all this rice."

Roxanne laughed and stood up. "Well, you might be right. Too, we need to save our energy for Mr. Arthur's."

On the fourteenth after breakfast, we went downtown to the museum. Roxanne had arranged to work the night shift, so we were set. We spent hours cutting out baseball caps ranging from pea-size to the size of a grapefruit, depending on the picture. We must've made at least a thousand. By the time we decided to quit, my back hurt, I had blisters from the scissors and my eyes were stinging. And after all our work, Mr. Arthur didn't even seem to care.

A couple of times he looked around at the walls and grinned, but he never said thank you or that he appreciated all our effort.

"We've wasted a whole day," I complained. "I thought this was supposed to be a celebration."

Roxanne sat on the floor cross-legged and barefoot, still pasting on a few caps. I was lying on my back with my sore hands crossed over my chest. "What's a celebration?" she asked. "It's just something that when you remember it, you feel good. I don't know about you, Jesse, but I'll never forget this day. It'll be a good memory."

"Are you sure you won't remember it in your nightmares?" I said, checking out one blister that was puffed up like a bubble. Roxanne had broken two fingernails, which she'd taped back on with masking tape until she could glue them right. Still, she wasn't one bit upset.

"Sometimes when you do something nice, it's like planting flower seeds in a desert. Maybe nobody but the birds and clouds will notice. But the world at least has a little more beauty. And it needs all it can get, don't you think?"

"I can't see spending all day working for a bird or a cloud," I told her. "Cutting about a million caps and sticking them on pictures is the stupidest thing I've ever heard of. Besides counting grains of rice, that is."

"I don't think it matters what you're doing, Jesse. It's really all about love. And love can't ever be stupid."

I turned and saw Mr. Arthur standing at the doorway holding his two-headed chicken wrapped in a doll blanket. He smiled at us. Roxanne dropped her glue bottle and turned up the radio. She grabbed Mr. Arthur and waltzed around the room with him.

"What a cute baby you have," she told him, nodding down at his chicken, which was wedged between them. He smiled just like it was a real baby.

While they danced around the room, I thought back about Mr. Arthur and his wife, Ruby. They used to pay me to do chores after school, and I had dusted the orange, twisted beak and black glass eyes on that chicken's good head more times than I could count. The deformed head was more like a big white sprout that grows on a potato, but Mr. Arthur swore it was the real thing. He'd ordered the chicken from a catalog and he was so proud.

Now it was his baby. Maybe he even thought it was Elma.

The song ended, but Mr. Arthur wanted to dance again, so he and Roxanne started back around the room.

After the two-headed chicken and his wax pieces, Mr. Arthur's favorite exhibit was a little picture that he kept behind a purple velvet curtain about the size of a postcard. You were supposed to be sixteen years old to look, but he let me since I worked there so much.

It was a black-and-white photograph taken in a dimestore picture booth of a woman who had five breasts. The top pair were the normal ones and were covered by her blouse, but she lifted the bottom part of her blouse to show another pair. Each one, about three or four inches on either side of her navel, looked exactly like a baby's, small and flat, completely undeveloped. The card under the picture said she had another one under her arm, so that made five in all.

Every time I dusted, I peeked at that woman. Her face looked so tired, her eyes like empty sockets. She sat there just gazing at nothing, waiting for the camera to click so she could get her money and go home.

"That's sad," I'd told him. "Why did you buy it?" He'd said he'd found it in a big fishbowl of pictures at an auction, that he liked to show people things that made them wonder or ask questions.

"There's way too many answers in the world," he'd said. "'If people can find just one thing that's a mystery, maybe they'd slow down, not think they know so much. People don't want to think about the universe, they just want to use it."

"Aren't you using that woman?" I'd asked.

Mr. Arthur had stopped to think, working his mouth like he was chewing a tough piece of steak. He'd twirled his mustache and made a clicking noise with his tongue.

Ruby had been dusting the glass eyes of Charlie, a buffalo that stood in a corner. She'd looked over at Mr. Arthur to see how he'd answer.

"That's a tough one, Jess. Yep, you ask the best questions. I think if you keep that up, you'll go a long way in life."

"Mr. Arthur," I'd said, frustrated, "you didn't answer my question."

"Right!" he'd said. "It's the nature of the universe. Full of questions. Couldn't figure it out if you tried."

Roxanne and Mr. Arthur's song ended, and Roxanne flopped down on the floor. Mr. Arthur dropped his chicken and wandered into the next room. I thought it was time to go home, but Roxanne had another idea.

"Elma," she hollered up the basement stairs, "could you come down here and take a picture?"

While Elma was getting the camera, Roxanne headed over to the baseball section. "You guys don't mind me borrowing a few caps, do you?" she said to the wax figures in uniform. She got a cap for herself, me, Mr. Arthur, and five extra, one for each of the disciples and Jesus.

"We're getting our picture taken!" she said, putting the caps on everybody.

Pretty soon Elma came down, and when she saw us all lined up at the Lord's table, she blew a huge bubble with her bubble gum and said she needed a cigarette. "I've never seen such a irreligious thing," she griped. "This picture's gonna cost two dollars instead of the regular, which is one dollar." Then she added, "Daddy, get yourself out of that picture!"

Mr. Arthur put his hands on Peter's shoulders and shook his head. He wasn't going anywhere, and since Elma's soap opera was about to come on and she didn't want to miss it, she sighed real big and took our picture. It came rolling out of the camera a few seconds later, and while she headed back up the stairs we all waited for the picture to show up real good.

"I'll send this to you when you get settled, Mr. Arthur," Roxanne said. "But maybe it'll be a long time yet before they have a place for you."

When it was time to go home, Roxanne hugged Mr. Arthur and I did too. His body felt bony like a baby bird's. Roxanne rushed outside without even saying goodbye. She said she didn't believe in it.

I don't know if I agree. I always wished I could have said goodbye to William III.

On the way home Roxanne said, "I have a good feeling here in Ida. I feel connected to something, sort of held in close, like a hug."

We watched the sun go down on the way home. The air glowed orange and gold, and with me and Roxanne and the sun and the giant oaks shining black against the sky and home getting closer and closer, I kind of understood what Roxanne meant by feeling connected to things.

By the time we got to the trailer park, the sky had

turned a soft gray, like the fur on a cat. All the dirty smudges on our front door showed up in the dusk, and I noticed for the first time how bad the paint was peeling around the windows. Even outside I could smell the pinto beans Mama was cooking. But in spite of it all, I was glad to be home.

CHAPTER 6

New people don't come to Ida all that much, and when they do, people notice. That's how it was with Roxanne and that's how it was with the new girl at school. For Frankenstein, she was just somebody new to pick on. At first I didn't care because I figured now he'd leave me alone. But Debbie Bartacelli was different.

The first time I saw her was in English, which is the first period of the day. She was sitting in the desk in front of mine and she was all hunched over with her head bent almost to the desktop, reading a book. Her auburn hair covered her face like a blanket.

When kids started coming into class, they pointed and whispered, but she never looked up. Not even when Mrs. Noble shuffled into the room with a flag clenched between her teeth, carrying about ten books with a coffee cup on top and pencils sticking out behind each ear like missiles. Pressed between her chin and her chest, she had a huge map of Greece or somewhere, and her glasses balanced on the tip of her nose like scales. I expected Frankenstein to make a stupid comment, and he did.

"Watch out behind you, Mrs. Noble!" He hollered like there was a fire or something. She jumped a little, but managed to hang on to everything except for an ink pen, which popped out of one of the books and hit the floor. It rolled all the way to Debbie's desk and stopped.

Mrs. Noble set her stuff down and spit out the flag. She looked right at the new girl.

"Would you bring me my pen, please?"

"Sure," the girl said, jumping out of her seat. That's when we all saw Debbie Bartacelli's face.

It was almost like someone had cut her face in half from her hairline to her chin, then put it back together—only one side didn't quite match the other. Like in home economics class when we had to learn to match plaids, and somebody would always put the stripe next to the check instead of next to the matching stripe.

One of her eyes was slightly higher than the other one. And one side of her lips turned up a little in a kind of grin while the other side stretched down. Nobody said a word as she walked to the front, but when she got back to her seat, I saw a folded note on top of her book. It had "NEW GIRL" scrawled on it with a curly border. She ignored it at first, listening to Mrs. Noble talk about an article she'd read in the newspaper about a dog that could read. Then she opened it.

Someone had written in big green letters "Welcome

Frog Face!" She stared at it for a few seconds then put it inside her desk. She bent her head way down again and sat just as still as one of the light fixtures, barely even breathing.

I glanced around. Mrs. Noble was standing on her chair trying to put the flag in its holder. She was saying how glad she was to have the new girl, Debbie Bartacelli, in our class.

Then I noticed Frankenstein smirking and scribbling on a piece of paper with a green marker. I ripped a piece of paper from my spiral and wrote a note to Debbie. "I'm the girl behind you. My name is Jesse. I know the nerd who wrote the note. We'll get even!" I tossed the note over her shoulder onto her desk.

She brushed it off onto the floor. When the bell rang, I tried to talk to her. "Hey, Debbie," I said, "I saw that note about the frog. I know who did it."

She turned and glared at me. "Who said I needed your help?" she snapped. All of a sudden she reminded me of one of those big turtles Doris Ray finds out in the backyard. No matter how cute she dresses them up in doll dresses, they're still turtles and they'll snap at you when they get a chance.

I figured she probably thought I wrote the note about the frog, but after a while I decided, so what if she does? I don't need friends, especially ones like her. The rest of the day whenever I saw her, I pretended she wasn't there.

The next day in English, I didn't even look at Debbie Bartacelli. Frankenstein seemed to be ignoring her, too —that is, until we started in on *The Odyssey*. Mrs. Noble was reading aloud the part where the Cyclops, a one-eyed giant, eats up all Odysseus's men.

Frankenstein interrupted Mrs. Noble. "Did he eat their bones, too? What about the fingernails and hair?" He made a crunching noise at the back of his throat.

Mrs. Noble looked up, letting her glasses slide to the end of her nose. She said she imagined the giant ate each one in a single bite, kind of like popcorn. "Now, let's continue," she said, and she began to read.

"How big was this Cyclops dude?" Frankenstein interrupted again.

Mrs. Noble was probably counting to ten under her breath, but she answered him. "Well, now, Franklin, I suspect he must have been quite large." The class snickered, but Mrs. Noble didn't flinch. "He was at least as big as the water tower. Now, may I continue? And I'd like you to write down any further questions. I'll be happy to answer them. After school."

Frankenstein scrunched down into his chair and sulked. He pulled out his spiral notebook and started drawing.

He wrote "THE BRIDE OF CYCLOPS" in huge letters, decorating each one with a colored pencil. Underneath the title, he sketched a drawing of a girl. It looked exactly like Debbie, her crooked face peering out of a bride's veil. I didn't like her, either, but it made my blood boil to see him be so mean.

"Give me that," I whispered across the row. He stuck his pencil through one of the holes in the side of the paper and twirled it around. Mrs. Noble didn't even notice. She was definitely in the Cyclops world and wouldn't be coming out any time soon.

"They seized the beam of olive, sharp at the end, and leaned on it into the eye," Mrs. Noble boomed.

I knew any minute Frankenstein's Bride of Cyclops would fly off his pencil and the whole class would be laughing.

"Mrs. Noble," I said. She was still a million miles off.

"His eye sizzled about the beam of olive . . . ," she read, emphasizing the word *sizzled* like they do on sausage commercials.

"Mrs. Noble," I repeated. She finally looked up just as Frankenstein stopped twirling the paper.

"This better be important, Jesse," she warned. "Odysseus is just about to tell the Cyclops who he is."

"Well, uh . . . ," I said, not knowing for sure what I was going to do, but knowing that Frankenstein had to be stopped. I got up, grabbed the paper off his desk, folded it so no one would see and carried it to the front.

"Here," I whispered. I walked back to my seat feeling like a fool.

Mrs. Noble opened the paper. "I'll see you after class, Mr. Harris," she said, looking straight at Frankenstein.

Later at lunch in the cafeteria line, everybody was talking about Debbie—that is, until she walked up. Margaret Jane Anderson said real slow in Debbie's face, "Would—you—care—to—join—us—at—our—table—for—lunch?"

Debbie stared right at her and said just as slowly, "Just — because — my — face — is — messed — up — does—not—mean—I'm—stupid!"

Margaret Jane turned as bright red as a strawberry.

Debbie continued, "Thanks—anyway—but—I'm—eating—with—Jesse."

Debbie could sure take care of herself. I'd never try to protect her again. She could hold her own with Frankenstein and maybe it would be fun to see her do it.

CHAPTER 7

Anybody who thought Debbie Bartacelli was going to be shy was wrong. Anybody who thought she wasn't smart was doubly wrong. In two weeks she published the first edition of *The Icon*, Eli Whitney's first and probably last newspaper.

There was a page of articles:

"A Comparison of Eighth-Grade Mating Behavior with the Bugling of the American Elk" (a discussion of the characteristics of each), "Asteroid Destroys Dinosaurs" (how a giant asteroid hit the Yucatan peninsula sixty-five million years ago and may have led to the dinosaur extinction), "Chickadee Chokes on Balloon" (on the dangers of releasing masses of helium balloons), and "Do Fingernails Grow after Death?" (insights from a mortician's journal).

Everybody thought it was pretty weird, especially how

underneath the name of the paper Debbie added the quote, "I only gave you an onion, nothing but a tiny little onion, that's all, that's all!"

At the very end of the paper she offered a five-dollar reward for the answer to the question: "In what piece of literature would one find the devil in a cube of ice?"

Nobody in Eli Whitney had ever seen anyone quite like Debbie. She had a lot of intelligence and a lot of courage, which made Mr. Huber, our principal, suspicious.

The day after the paper came out, he called her into his office, and she told our whole English class about it.

"The poor man's scared to death I'm going to stir up the status quo, which of course is exactly what I plan to do. And I need people to help. Volunteers?"

Nobody said a word.

Finally one hand went up.

"Franklin?" Debbie asked. "Can you write?"

"No," he answered. "I can draw. I'll be the cartoonist."

Everybody groaned. But Debbie said, "Good. I'll take you. Anyone else?"

I stared at my desk. Then Mrs. Noble cleared her throat and said, "Thank you, Jesse. You're a good writer."

I looked up. "I didn't raise my hand!"

"But you will help, won't you?" Debbie said, staring at me. I couldn't tell if she was frowning or smiling. "You're not afraid, are you?"

"I'm not afraid," I said, "it's not that. I just don't want to." Actually, I was afraid—not of Mr. Huber, but of being part of a group made up of Frankenstein and Debbie Bartacelli with the crooked face. It was too much.

"It's time to start class now," Mrs. Noble announced. "You can have your newspaper meetings before school."

When the bell rang, Debbie brushed by my desk. "See you tomorrow at seven-fifteen. Don't be late," she said, just as if I'd agreed to come.

The next morning at seven-fifteen Debbie didn't seem a bit surprised that I showed up. Frankenstein was there, too. The misfits, I thought, ready to begin. Still, it was something to do and I was curious. It might be better than Saturday-night wrestling on TV. Debbie and Frankenstein, Round One.

Debbie stood at the front of the room and spoke loudly, as if the room was full of reporters. "First off, you all should know," she began, taking off her thick glasses and rubbing the scars around her eyes, "according to Mr. Huber, I can keep the paper as long as I don't get too controversial. I think that means to leave out God, sex, and four-letter words. Subversive ideas are okay."

Mrs. Noble, who was working at her desk, chuckled.

"What are subversive ideas?" Frankenstein wanted to know. "The kind perverts have?"

"I was being facetious," Debbie answered.

"I thought you were just being weird," Frankenstein said. We hadn't met five minutes and things were already falling apart.

"For your information," Debbie began, "the word *subversive* has to do with ideas that are formed with the intent of overthrowing the government, of which, I'm sure, you are quite capable. And *facetious* means funny, which you are not."

"I'm not staying." Frankenstein stood and headed for the door.

"Sit down," Debbie commanded. Strangely, he stopped. "You've got a lot of talent. I saw that Bride of Cyclops thing. You know, the picture that was supposed to be me? It looked just like me. And it was funny. Now sit down and shut up. You're the *Icon* cartoonist and you're not allowed to quit."

Frankenstein stood there looking confused. This newspaper idea was going to be more interesting than I had first thought.

"So how are we paying for this paper?" I asked. "It'll cost money to get it printed." I thought it was time for an intelligent question.

"My mother," Debbie answered. She told us how her face had gotten messed up in a car wreck when she was ten and how her mother had been killed in the crash. "My mother was a journalist, and she left a sum of money for my education. I'm using some of it for *The Icon*."

Everybody knew Debbie lived with her aunt, who owned the only beauty shop in town. Her father, a professor in language studies, was traveling in Europe. "I'm between surgeries," she added, "and *The Icon* gives me a place to focus my nervous energy."

"What kind of name is Icon?" I asked.

"An icon is a symbol. It works kind of like a window. You look through it to see something more important on the other side."

"Weird," Frankenstein said. For once, I had to agree with him.

Later, I told Roxanne about our first meeting and all about Debbie. We were sitting in the tearoom, which is what she called her living room. There wasn't a couch since she always said furniture tied her down too much. She had on this purple satin robe with a map of Guam embroidered on the back, and we were eating popcorn and drinking hot peppermint tea.

"She knows he wrote the Frog Face note and drew the Bride of Cyclops picture, and she still wants Frankenstein on the paper," I said.

Roxanne sipped at her tea slowly. She stared past me in deep thought. "Debbie's turned out so well. What I mean is, in spite of the accident. On top of that, she has to wear her pain all the time for everyone to see."

"And for creeps like Frankenstein to make fun of," I added.

"Frankenstein." Roxanne shook her head. "What kind of name is that?"

"One that fits," I answered. "We don't usually call him that to his face, though."

"It just seems so cruel," she said softly, tracing her finger around the rim of her teacup.

"What? Debbie or Frankenstein?"

"Both, I guess."

"Believe me, Roxanne, Frankenstein's name is perfect for him. And Debbie, she can hold her own."

"Jesse?" Roxanne's face knotted into a frown.

"Yeah? Are you sick?"

Roxanne ran her fingers through her hair. "Some things in life just never seem to fit right."

I didn't understand her at all, and for once Doris Ray came knocking at the right time.

"It's my sister. I gotta go."

Roxanne said she'd see me tomorrow, and when I left she was still sitting on the floor in a patch of light from the window.

CHAPTER 8

It was at the Laundromat a couple of weeks later that Roxanne told me her secret. We were washing towels and other stuff, and she said, "Jesse, you know I've been married before."

"Yeah, to Robert, right?"

"He was my second husband. I was married once before him."

I must have looked surprised, which I was, since she'd never mentioned another husband before. She looked at me real hard for a moment and then turned away.

"We got married when we were still in high school," Roxanne said, sorting out colors in piles on the floor. "I was barely sixteen years old. We didn't even have to. We were so much in love, Jesse. I've never been in love like that since then."

"Couldn't you be in love without getting married?"

Barely sixteen wasn't that much older than me. I couldn't picture it.

"I lived in a little town, smaller than Ida. Johnny, that was his name, lived way out on a farm in the country. We couldn't see each other much without being married, so we ran off and did it."

Roxanne poured in the detergent, and for the first time I noticed a thin silver-and-turquoise ring on her right hand.

"We lived with his grandparents. They're the ones who raised him. I packed up all my stuffed animals and moved right into his bedroom."

I backed up against the washing machine so that I could feel it vibrate. "Wasn't that kind of strange sleeping in a bedroom right there in the same house with his grandparents?" Roxanne understood exactly what I was thinking.

"We slept outside a lot," she said, hoisting herself up to sit on the machine. "We made love on an old mattress Johnny dragged way out by the cornfield. Have you ever been in the country at night, Jesse? Have you ever been in total darkness?"

"Once," I said, "when we went to Carlsbad Caverns. They turned out the lights, and we couldn't even see our own hands." That was the summer after William III died, and when it got dark, I felt Mama next to me. She was shaking all over and she cried out, "Please turn on the lights, please!" When they did, she had her face in her hands and she was sobbing.

"Being in the dark with Johnny was like living inside a dream," Roxanne said. "A dream where you don't remember the pictures, but the feeling you never forget. You know, Jesse, sometimes I can't even see Johnny's face or hear his voice, but I feel what it was like lying next to him in the dark."

I knew exactly what she meant. William III's face wasn't real clear to me anymore, either. But I can't forget how soft he was or that powdery smell after his bath.

"What about your parents? They let you stay married? Mine would throw a fit."

"I was one of eleven kids," Roxanne said. "Not the oldest or the youngest, just somewhere in the middle. My daddy could barely put a pot of beans on the table. Mama always had morning sickness. Does that answer your question?"

I tried to picture Roxanne being part of a big family. It was hard.

"Anyway, about Johnny," Roxanne said. "He was beautiful. Tight brown body. Hard, muscular—and smooth. A highway in the desert, Jesse. You hear women say they want a hairy man? They never had Johnny."

I looked around to see if anyone else had come into the Laundromat, and I was glad they hadn't. "So what was the problem?" I asked.

She propped her elbows on her knees and thought. "Johnny's grandparents had high hopes for him before I came along. They wanted him to go to college, be a doctor."

"What happened?"

Roxanne sighed and slid down off the washer.

"It just wasn't right, Jesse. He should've died in a war. Or fallen off a mountain or a wild horse. There's so many better ways it could've happened. He shouldn't have fallen from an old windmill that didn't even work anymore."

"Were you with him?" I asked.

She shook her head. "That's the bad part. We'd had this big argument about something real silly. I can't even remember what it was about. But I got mad, threw all my stuffed animals in a pillowcase and headed out the door."

"And it happened while you were gone?"

Roxanne nodded. "He went out late that night and climbed to the top of the windmill. It was real cloudy, which made it extra dark. He must've stepped on some wood that was rotted and slipped. They found his body on the ground when the sun came up."

"That's terrible," I said.

"The idea of losing what could have been, of losing all our dreams for the future, that's the worst thing. And then there was something else." Roxanne hesitated. She lifted the lid on the washer and watched the clothes spin around and around to a stop.

"I was pregnant."

"Oh," I said, thinking that was even worse than being married so young.

"I wanted to take care of the baby and be a good mother, but I knew I couldn't. I figured I had a chance to do the best thing I could ever do in my whole life." She said the words like she'd said them to herself a thousand times: they were worn smooth as rocks in a river.

"It was the hardest thing in the world. I gave my baby away."

"Couldn't his grandparents have helped you?"

"They never knew. Johnny didn't even know yet. Besides, they didn't like me, and they were old, way too old for a little bitty baby. So I left. Right after we buried Johnny."

I helped Roxanne put all the wet stuff in a dryer and she finished her story.

"I didn't have anything to wear to a funeral. I'd never been to one. And the preacher asked me what songs I wanted. I only knew one funeral song." Roxanne started singing. "Swing Low—Sweet Chariot—Comin' for to carry me home—Sw-i-i-i-ng low—Sweet Char-i-o-ot, Comin' for to carry me home. . . ." Roxanne's song floated around the Laundromat as soft and fluttery as cotton.

"Lord, Jesse. You should have seen me at that funeral. I had some black patent spike heels Johnny loved, so I wore them and this square-dance dress that my best friend loaned me. It was bright turquoise with silver rick-rack all over. You had to wear this big net cancan underneath to make the skirt stand out. Like this."

Roxanne held her arms out at her sides and twirled around, almost falling over the detergent box.

"Be careful," I warned her.

Ignoring me, she kept on. "I thought it was the most gorgeous dress I'd ever seen."

Roxanne finally stopped twirling, and I stretched out on four of the plastic chairs next to the dryers.

"Johnny's grandmother told me I shouldn't dress like that for a funeral. But I said I wanted to look real pretty for my husband."

She paused, twisting her ring. "It rained at the cemetery. The ground was already wet because it'd been raining all week, and by the time the last prayer was over it really started pouring down. Everybody was running to their cars, and I did too, but those heels of mine stuck into the mud like tent stakes and I fell forward on the grass, right on my face. That cancan and skirt flipped up to my head like the trunk lid on a car. Johnny's grandmother was mortified."

"I would've died," I said. And I meant it.

Roxanne laughed. "That's when I decided that what you wear underneath is more important than what you wear on the outside."

"How can you laugh about something so horrible?" I asked her.

"Oh, I don't know. I guess I figure there's enough to cry about in the here and now without crying over the then, too."

"So after the funeral, did you go back to your parents'?"

"No. I moved off to another town, got a job. The doctor there knew a couple who wanted a baby more than anything in the world, and the wife couldn't ever have one herself. They were educated, had plenty of money, a stable life. I never met them, but they promised to love my baby. They also promised to let my child know something about its heritage, which is Cherokee on my mother's side of the family."

"Do you think if you hadn't gotten mad, Johnny would still be alive?"

Roxanne bent down to pick up the laundry basket.

She walked closer to the dryer and stood there watching the load of towels slow to a stop.

"I don't know. Life is crazy," she said.

I wanted her to say more than that. To explain how things didn't work that way. But she didn't.

The towels were almost too hot to touch, but Roxanne hugged an armful up next to her chest. She buried her nose in them.

"Ummmm," she said. "Don't you love how towels smell when they come out of the dryer?"

I couldn't get my mind off Johnny. I had to know it wasn't Roxanne's fault. "It was dumb for him to climb on a windmill in the middle of the night," I said.

Roxanne folded the last towel and looked at me. "He'd done it before. We both used to climb up there and look at the stars at night, and sometimes in the day we'd climb up there so we could see the whole world. But his grandparents thought it was my fault."

I shook my head.

"I only have one thing left of Johnny. His hand. You've seen that plaster hand in my bedroom?"

I said I'd noticed it before, but I was thinking about the baby.

"What was it? A boy or a girl?"

"It was one of the two," Roxanne teased. Then she got real serious. "I never touched my baby. I was afraid to. I thought if I held it, I might not ever let go, and I had to."

"You did the right thing," I said. "Now, which was it, a son or a daughter?"

Roxanne turned her face away from me. "I don't want to say, Jesse. Not yet, anyway."

I walked around and faced her to see if she was kidding. But she wasn't.

"If I could hug my baby, just once, it'd last me the rest of my life," she whispered.

"Do you know where it is?"

"The records were sealed, but I know. Don't ask how. I just know."

"Do you want it back? That wouldn't be possible, would it?"

"No, that wouldn't be best for anyone. Just a hug, that's all I want."

"You could go there, Roxanne." It wasn't like William III. She still had a chance.

"Jesse?" Roxanne was barely breathing. "Why do you think I moved to Ida?"

CHAPTER 9

Frankenstein sat all by himself on the front steps of the school. He had his head on his knees and I could hear him breathing kind of loud, as if he was asleep. Bent down like that, he didn't look so mean. I planned to walk past real quiet, but he raised up and grumbled something.

"Hi," I said. "I'm here early for the newspaper."

He looked around. The schoolyard was empty except for the two of us. "Did somebody ask you why you're here early?" he snarled.

I started up the steps to the door and added that I just wondered if he was there to work on the paper, too.

"You gotta be kidding," he said. "I'm not getting within ten feet of Frog Face or her stupid *Ick-on*."

"It's *Icon*. And why do you have to call her that? What's she ever done to you?"

"She pollutes the air." He blurted the words like they were darts he was throwing at a target.

"She can't help her face," I said. "Her mother was killed in that accident. Don't you have any feelings?"

"Yeah, I have feelings. I feel it was a shame she survived. If she hadn't, I wouldn't have to look at her."

He jumped up, grabbed the tree branch overhanging the steps and swung himself to the sidewalk.

"Have you looked in the mirror lately?" I asked. "Try it. Maybe you can understand why everybody calls you Frankenstein." I'd never said the name to his face, and I couldn't believe I was doing it now, but I'd had enough.

He didn't say anything. I wanted him to, but he didn't. He just sat down on the bottom step and put his head back on his knees.

I went on up the steps. I had definitely won, but it sure didn't feel like it.

"You look like you just saw a ghost," Debbie said when I walked into Mrs. Noble's room.

"More like a monster," I told her.

Mrs. Noble looked up from her desk in the back and asked, "Jesse, do you happen to know a word for 'small shark'? It's got four letters and it starts with a *t* and ends with *e*."

"I don't guess Franklin Harris fits, does it?" I could see Franklin swimming through the water, his teeth bared and dripping with blood. Looking for trouble.

Mrs. Noble must not have heard me. "How about a city in Iran, three letters, starts with a Q, and the second letter can't be *u*."

"Sorry, I haven't taken world geography yet," I told her.

"*Tope*—any of several small sharks," Debbie read from the dictionary. "It can also mean to drink alcohol excessively or a Buddhist shrine. Take your pick."

"Perfecto," Mrs. Noble exclaimed. "That makes *Qom* for the city. Now I can start my day." She folded the newspaper and dropped it into the trash.

"How can you just throw away all that work?" I asked her.

She looked up at me over her glasses, then took them off and let them hang from the chain she wears around her neck.

"It's all in the challenge," she said. "The end result's nice, but it's not the important part."

"Well, I'll tell you a challenge. Franklin Harris. He was sitting on the steps when I came in. Tried to pick a fight, as usual."

"You know, he's really a very smart young man," Mrs. Noble said.

"Smart-mouthed," I answered.

Debbie was sitting at the computer typing. "We need him on the paper. He can draw."

"He's a jerk. A troublemaker. You don't want him," I said.

"Ummm." Debbie reached for the page coming out of the printer. "Here, edit this," she said, handing me an article titled "Oklahoma Farmer Harvests Largest Peanut Ever Recorded."

"Why do you write all these science things?" I asked.

"Because girls are not supposed to be interested in

science, but of course we are," she said. "I'm not sure an article about a giant peanut exactly qualifies as science, though."

I looked over her shoulder and read aloud the title of the next article she was typing. "Protozoa Suspected of Sexual Activity."

"I thought Mr. Huber wanted nothing to do with sex," I said.

Debbie laughed. "That's probably true. But I think in this article the mention of protozoa will throw him."

"We studied protozoa for a whole week in Mr. Butterfield's class before you got here. They're just little squiggly things. They don't have any . . . well, you know," I said.

"Sex organs?" Debbie glanced up at me, but she kept on typing.

"I just meant protozoa aren't exactly people," I said.

"No, but some scientists think they really do reproduce sexually, that it takes two and not just one as they had always assumed," she explained.

She stopped typing.

"After I got hurt," she said, "I was in a coma for a few weeks. When I woke up, I wanted to know where I was and I asked for my mother."

I looked into her dark eyes. "You didn't know about the wreck?"

"I couldn't remember anything about the accident. For a long time afterward I had nightmares about flying through the air toward a huge tree trunk. But I always woke up just before I hit anything."

Debbie has long scars that run like a crooked creek

down her arm and end up in a tangled mass of scar on her hand. While she talked, she rubbed the twisted skin near her fingers.

"When my father told me about my mother, I was furious. I threw my food against the wall every time they tried to get me to eat—oatmeal, scrambled eggs, milk shakes. I screamed at everyone. I hated everybody."

"Well, you had a right. You'd lost your mother."

"The thing is," she said, "Franklin must be angry about something. He acts like I did."

"Give me a break, Debbie. Believe me, his parents have given him everything he's ever wanted. Have you seen the house he lives in?" The Harrises live in the biggest house in Ida, a two-story with elegant white columns. It looks like something you'd see on television or in the movies.

"I know where he lives. Still, there must be some reason for his behavior." Debbie reached to the floor for her purse. She took out her wallet and opened it to a picture of a striking woman with sleek blond hair and piercing blue eyes. "My mother," she said.

I glanced away, hoping Debbie hadn't noticed my surprise.

"You don't think I look like her, do you?" she said. "Well, what do you expect?" she asked, touching her scarred face.

"So how'd you get over being mad? Have a brain transplant? That's probably the only hope for Frankenstein Harris."

"No brain transplant, that's for sure," Debbie said. "I don't think it was any one thing. I guess I just decided to accept what had happened. It's part of who I am, Debbie Bartacelli."

"Well, I don't think Frankenstein will be that sensible, not without the brain transplant, that is." I was tired of talking about poor Franklin Harris. In my opinion, no excuse would be good enough for him, and for a change I was glad when the bell rang and it was time to go to class.

CHAPTER 10

If Frankenstein's eyes had shot poison, I'd be dead. I passed him at the door to English and went on to my seat and pulled out my homework. As usual, he dragged his feet all the way to his chair, then dropped his books on the floor like a bomb. He stretched his legs under the seat in front of him, which pushed his desk back and caused all the ones behind him to knock together. Then he sat there whistling between his teeth, real soft, like a teakettle after the fire's been turned off.

I put my head down, listening to the kids come in for class. Pretty soon, I wasn't thinking about anything but Roxanne and our talk at the Laundromat. She hadn't wanted to talk about it anymore that day, and she'd asked me to keep our conversation to myself.

"I don't generally believe in secrets," she'd said. "They can fester up in you and cause all kinds of problems. But this is the kind of thing that can't be let out. It could hurt people."

I felt good that she trusted me, and I wouldn't let her down, no matter what. Besides, I didn't have a good enough friend to tell.

In the distance, I could hear Mrs. Noble's voice, but it seemed real far away. I put my hand over my eyes to make it look like I was reading in my literature book like everyone else, then I went back to thinking about Roxanne. I was thinking about all the babies I knew and trying to match their looks to Roxanne's when I realized what an idiot I was being. If she'd been around seventeen when the baby was born, the kid would be around thirteen or fourteen now, probably a student in Eli Whitney. Maybe even somebody in my class. I'd never heard talk about anyone being adopted, though.

Then it hit me. Debbie and Roxanne were both new in town. And they were both redheads with dark eyes. *Impossible*, I told myself. Instead, I was hoping it would be somebody like Rodney Grey, who's really cute and sits behind me in math. In a way, I could see Roxanne's cheekbones in his—or maybe it was his chin. I was about to look at each girl and boy, row by row, when I felt Mrs. Noble standing by my desk. I guess more time had passed than I'd realized.

"What page are we on, Jesse?"

I cleared my throat a couple of times and coughed.

"Jesse, what have you been doing? Counting sheep?" Mrs. Noble walked around my desk in her getting-your-attention walk.

"No ma'am," I said. "Uh, I was just sitting here thinking about—about Dr. Jekyll and Mr. Hyde." I hoped she'd appreciate the fact that I had literature on my mind.

"That's interesting." Mrs. Noble stood beside me so close I could smell her face powder and count the brown spots on her left hand. Her other hand was on my shoulder in her I'm-warning-you position.

"We were discussing Robert Burns's 'A Red, Red Rose,' Jesse," she said, squeezing my shoulder just a little. "Tell us, how did the poem remind you of Dr. Jekyll?" When Mrs. Noble asks a question, she expects an answer.

I glanced at Susan sitting next to me. She'd have her book open to the right page. She didn't let me down either. "It's about love. p. 214," she wrote real big on a piece of notebook paper so I could see.

I mouthed "Thanks," and thumbed through my book as fast as I could to the poem.

"Read the third and fourth stanzas for us, please, Jesse. Then explain the relationship between this poem and Dr. Jekyll and Mr. Hyde." Mrs. Noble was determined to make me pay for daydreaming.

She squeezed my shoulder again from her I-mean-business position.

> Till a' the seas gang dry, my dear,
> And the rocks melt wi' the sun:
> And I will love thee still, my dear,
> While the sands o' life shall run.

And fare thee weel, my only luve,
And fare thee weel a while!
And I will come again, my luve,
Though it were ten thousand mile.

I stopped and looked up at her.

"Go on," she said. "Explain."

"Well, the poem," I said, "is about love." I glanced over at Susan and she nodded. I looked at the words on the page. "And the person who loves would love someone until the rocks melted, which I guess means forever." I never have understood why poets don't just come right out and say what they mean.

"Go on," Mrs. Noble said again. Her hand, which was now on my desk, had big blue veins that stuck out like the rivers on a 3-D map.

"I guess someone must've lost track of the person they loved on account of they said they'd go ten thousand miles to find them," I said. *Like Roxanne.* Only I didn't say that aloud.

"And Dr. Jekyll?" Mrs. Noble wasn't going to give up. She stayed at my desk, towering over me like the Statue of Liberty, pressing for truth.

I tried to explain. "Dr. Jekyll, well, I felt sorry for him. I mean, he didn't really want his bad side to take over for good, but it finally did anyway. He couldn't do anything to stop it. I guess the story doesn't have love in it like the poem."

Mrs. Noble nodded. "It sounds as though you're saying that if someone had loved Dr. Jekyll until all the seas went dry, perhaps the good part might have survived, and perhaps it would have grown."

I didn't remember saying that at all, but Mrs. Noble was finally letting me off the hook, so I agreed. "Yes ma'am, I guess that's what I meant."

"Class," Mrs. Noble went on, "it's the attempt to join disparate parts of the world that enables us to create unity. Literature helps us learn to do that."

She walked up to the front again and I breathed a sigh of relief. I don't think anybody knew what in the heck Mrs. Noble was talking about, but I was saved, at least.

"Students, your homework for tomorrow is to write one hundred and fifty words about something or someone you love enough to travel ten thousand miles to see." Mrs. Noble ignored the groans in the classroom and told us to put away our books and get ready for the bell.

Most of us haven't traveled much more than a hundred miles from home. The air conditioner in our car's been broken for two summers, and I'd hate to go ten thousand feet with Mama and Daddy and all us kids packed in, but I wrote down the assignment and shut my book.

Maybe I'd go that far to see Roxanne if I had to. Or if it was possible, I'd go see William III.

CHAPTER 11

At suppertime I still had Roxanne on my mind, which is a miracle considering it's impossible to think at our table. We all sat down and Doris Ray, Jimmy, and Roy Dean fought over who got to say the prayer. Mama said they all three could have a turn, but Doris Ray started whining about how she ought to go first since she's older, and Roy Dean hollered and kicked his chair because he wanted to be first. Jimmy let out a wail that sounded just like something on *Wild Kingdom*, and Daddy said, "Jesse will be first, now everybody hush."

I said I didn't even want to pray at all, but everybody's head was bowed, so I said, "Dear God, if you're out there somewhere please make these kids shut up so we can have some peace and quiet and be able to eat. Amen."

Mama said, "Jesse, God does not appreciate a smart mouth."

"Maybe He has a sense of humor," I argued.

Daddy frowned. "Jesse, that's enough, or you'll go without dinner."

I said fine because I'd rather eat cat food than this smelly corned beef. Well, actually, I really didn't say it out loud, but I wished I could've.

Doris Ray got to pray next. She went on and on about a green-and-yellow-striped caterpillar she'd found out back and how she hoped God would make it into a butterfly by tomorrow, and please let it be a monarch. After she'd blessed the grass and trees and the President of the United States, Mama said, "That's real fine, Doris Ray."

Daddy said he hoped someone would remember to thank the good Lord for the food so that we could get it blessed and eat. Jimmy got to be next since he's five minutes older than Roy Dean. Being only three, he didn't know what to call everything, so he said, "Thank you for this brown stuff, and this green stuff, and this yellow stuff, and specially the bread." Roy Dean said the exact same thing and finally it was time to eat.

While the boys were sword fighting with their forks and Mama was talking about an okra recipe she wanted to try, I was thinking about Roxanne and the baby.

"Jesse! Jesse!" Mama interrupted my thoughts. "You're dumping salt all over your food."

Doris Ray giggled.

"Can I go over to Roxanne's?" I asked.

"Jesse, you've hardly eaten. Besides, I think you're

spending too much time with that girl—woman—whatever you want to call her."

"How about 'friend'? And why do you hate her so much?"

Mama looked at Daddy. "I don't hate her. It's her values, Jesse. The tattoo thing. Her influence on you."

"Mama, you don't even really know her. Roxanne's the kind of person who'd save a turtle in the middle of the road. Last week she stopped her car and moved one out of the way of traffic. It was one of those big ones like Doris Ray finds."

Doris Ray, being she's so crazy about turtles, bawled, "Oh, that poor little thing out in the middle of the road. A car could've squashed it dead. Oh, Lord." She carried on like the thing really had gotten squashed. I swear, Doris Ray never misses a chance to put on a show.

The twins banged their spoons on their plates. "We wanta see the turtle squashed! We wanta see the turtle squashed!"

"The turtle did not get squashed. Roxanne saved it. That was the point of the story!" It's impossible to say anything and really be heard at my house.

"May I please go," I begged. "I'll do the dishes as soon as I get home. And I'll get the kids' baths and put them to bed."

Mama sighed real big and said she guessed so, and I left.

I knocked on Roxanne's door and hollered that it was me, and she yelled to come on in.

"I'm in the kitchen," she said. "Iron my hair, will you?" Roxanne's the only person I've ever known who irons her hair. She said she got started in high school and never quit. Said Johnny used to do it for her, and Robert did, too, before he got mean.

I said I would, and she put her cheek on the ironing board and I combed her hair out almost to the end. I laid a dishtowel over it, then pressed it until all the curls straightened out.

"How's school?" she asked.

"Okay. We read this poem today," I said, ironing the ends one more time. "It was all about loving somebody until the sea dried up."

"That's what I like about the sea, Jesse. It's not going to dry up. One thing in life you can count on."

Roxanne turned her face toward me and I smoothed the other side of her hair.

"Anyway, I was thinking," I said. "About what you told me."

She knew exactly what I was talking about. "And you've been trying to figure out who it is, right?"

I nodded. "Sort of, I guess."

"When it's time, I'll let you know. For now, I just need you to be a friend. Hold off on the questions. Okay?"

I said all right and she turned the iron off and walked back over to me and gave me a big hug. "I always knew that you'd be the one to help me," she said.

I stiffened. "Help you what?"

"Get together with my kid. When it's time, that is. Okay?"

I said I guessed so, but it'd be hard since I didn't even know if it was male or female.

"You are so tense," she said, looking at my shoulders. "Try this. It really helps."

She stretched out on her back on the linoleum and pulled me down beside her. "Close your eyes," she said.

"Now start at your toes and tighten up as hard as you can. Go up to your ankles and knees, all the way up to the top of your head. Think of something that makes you mad."

That was easy.

"Now, pretend you're lying on the sand listening to the ocean. Your whole body is turning into ocean one part at a time. Relax and let each part go. You're becoming a wave; you're part of the whole big sea. Your last little toe is a part of the sea."

I looked over at Roxanne. She was as still as a drowned person. Her hair fanned around her head in long red ripples. The relaxation must've worked real good on her because I could barely see her breathing, just a slight rising right at her Liberty Bell.

Suddenly, Doris Ray was hollering at the door.

"Jesse, Je-e-e-sse-e, come ho-o-o-o-me."

I don't know why she can't just knock. She sounded like a tornado siren.

"Je-e-e-ss—" I opened the door, but she kept right on, her head tilted back, her mouth wide open like a baby bird's.

"Shut up, Doris Ray. I hear you," I told her. She was wearing one of my old Sunday dresses, a real tacky one the color of lima beans. The hem drooped almost to her ankles and one whole piece of lace, torn from the ruffles on a sleeve, strung down to her waist. Plus she had on a pair of Mama's high heels on the wrong feet. "You look pathetic," I said.

"Mama said for you to come home. Right now. You have to help put us to bay-ud."

"Bed," I told her. "It's got one syllable, *bed*."

"What's she doing?" Doris Ray pointed around the door at Roxanne who was still lying on the floor.

"She's trying to be the ocean. And she can't do it with you talking to her."

Roxanne sat up. "Oh, hi, Doris Ray," she said. "I love your outfit."

"Thanks," Doris Ray answered with a grin. "Jesse thinks it's dumb. Are you the ocean?"

"I'm the essence of it, sweetie pie," Roxanne said.

Oh, brother, I thought.

"And that dress! Jesse doesn't know what's in, does she? You and me, we have class!" Roxanne said.

Doris Ray stuck her tongue out at me.

"Come on," I said, grabbing her by the hand. "Let's go."

At home, after I did the dishes, Mama said for me to read the bedtime stories, which just about takes forever. There's gotta be one for Jimmy, one for Roy Dean, one for Doris Ray, and one for everybody together. I had another idea.

"Let's read *The Water Babies*. Four pages for each of you." They didn't seem to mind, so I started reading. It wasn't that bad because it's still one of my favorite stories. The dirty little chimney sweep who's covered in soot wants to be clean, so he slips into the sea and swims to the land of the water babies.

"Read the nasty eft part," Roy Dean and Jimmy said together. They like to hear about the efts, and Doris Ray loves the little water wings that sprout out of the babies' ribs.

To be a water baby seemed like the best thing ever to me—all fun and play, not a worry in the world. *Maybe that's how it is for William III*, I thought. *Maybe he's a water baby*.

After the story and the baths, I went on to bed. That is, Doris Ray and I did, since we have to share a bed.

"You cannot, absolutely not, be a butterfly in bed," I told her.

"Can I be a kangaroo?" she wanted to know.

"No," I said, and I drew an imaginary line down the center of the mattress to make her stay on her side.

"Good night," I told her. "Go to sleep."

"I want to cuddle up," she whined.

"Okay, just for one minute," and she snuggled up next to me.

"I'm a baby bunny," she said right before she fell asleep.

Later, when I heard Mama walking down the hall, I closed my eyes. Doris Ray was already asleep, purring like a kitten.

I felt Mama standing at the door for a long time, and in my mind I saw her—her blue flowered dress and that old yellow sweater, her thin brown hair. And the thing that stands out the most, her smooth face, almost like a baby's skin, and her cheeks that stay red without any blush makeup.

She stood at our door a good while. Then she went on

down the hall. I opened my eyes. From my bed I can see out the window into the sky. The full moon had gotten caught in the branches of the cottonwood tree. A big orange ball, waiting for someone to climb up there and pull it down. I looked at that moon for a long time, trying to see the mother and her baby, trying to see the moon pools Roxanne talked about. But I couldn't. It was just the moon stuck in the cottonwood tree.

Then I remembered my homework. One hundred fifty words on what I loved enough to travel ten thousand miles to see. I got up real slow so the springs wouldn't squeak and tiptoed out to the kitchen table.

CHAPTER 12

What I Would Travel Ten Thousand Miles to See
by
JESSE COWAN

When I was a kid, my favorite story was *The Water Babies* by Charles Kingsley. I loved that story. The water babies were the cutest things. I would travel ten thousand miles to see them.

They live in a fairy island far away in the sea and there are lots of sea caves where the water babies play. They love to swim in the water forests with the water monkeys and the water flowers. They play games with the lobsters and salmon and sometimes they ride on the backs of mermaids. Hundreds of water babies live in this deep part of the sea.

If I could go there, I would look for one special

water baby. He has light brown hair that's real thin and fine like corn silk. He's pretty chubby and has a small pink birthmark on the inside of his right knee. I'd go ten thousand miles to see him.

THE END

P.S. Mrs. Noble, there are 153 words in this essay. I hope that's not too many. Thank you, Jesse.

The day after I turned in my paper, a Saturday, Doris Ray was in the front yard flying around in her Christmas angel costume. Her idea of being an angel is to have everybody wait on her, so she was bossing Jimmy and Roy Dean around like crazy, making them pretend to bring her lemonade and cookies while she swooped through the drive kicking up gravel.

Her costume was just a plain white sheet with big paper wings Daddy made out of chicken wire and butcher paper, but Doris Ray put on like it was the real thing. You would've thought she had a real halo instead of just an embroidery hoop covered in gold tinsel.

At the Christmas program, she'd embarrassed our whole family. Mr. Scott had hauled all this hay from his barn into the church, and Doris Ray was supposed to stand in it in her angel costume and look down real sweet at Baby Jesus.

She did for a while. The kid reading the story, though, was taking forever and everybody was getting bored. Especially Doris Ray. Pretty soon, she reached down and picked up a long piece of straw. She fiddled with it awhile, then she put it between her fingers like a cigarette, brought it to her mouth and took a long drag. She took another puff, then another and another, pretending to blow smoke rings over the congregation. The whole church was snickering. Mama was mortified.

Doris Ray got in a lot of trouble and after that she said she'd never be an angel again, but she must've meant at church.

Anyway, the boys begged me to make Doris Ray stop bossing them, so I talked her into letting me help her up into the cottonwood tree.

"You can boss the whole world from up there," I told her. "Besides," I added, "maybe you'll see some other angels."

Roxanne says there really are angels, everywhere—in the trees, on the roofs, sitting on the hoods of cars, even lined up on the telephone wires. You just can't see them.

I want to know one thing. If that's true, why don't they do something besides sit around and watch people mess up all the time? They could've stopped Johnny from falling from that windmill. And they could've done something about Mrs. Arthur, and maybe even patched up Mr. Arthur's mind. Most of all, they could've done something about William III.

I mean, where were they when William III got sick? Where were they when Mama and Daddy wrapped him in cold wet towels trying to get his fever down? Where were they when he had to get hooked up to that breathing machine at the hospital? Where were they when I didn't pray the right words? The angels could've made the words right and taken them on up to Heaven before it was too late. But they didn't. I guess they just sat out on the crape myrtle doing nothing.

I hollered up at Doris Ray and asked her if she liked those weevil bugs that live in the tree. She stuck out her tongue.

"I'm gonna live up here ever and forever where I can watch the stars at night," she said. Then she said to bring her a hot dog because it was nearly suppertime.

I told her I thought angels were supposed to eat ambrosia.

She started whining and carrying on that she didn't like "brosia," and she wanted a hot dog and chocolate milk with a cherry in it.

Doris Ray is plain spoiled. I said if she didn't hush I'd just throw some birdseed up there and she'd have to make do. So she shut up.

I went on in and Mama said for me to get the hamburger started so we could have tacos for supper. "I hope angels will eat tacos," I said.

She gave me a funny look, but I didn't say anything else. I took out the taco shells and chopped up some lettuce and tomatoes and grated the cheese. No way would I fix Doris Ray a wiener. Mama wouldn't be about to let her eat in the tree while the rest of us sat at the table. But in a way I wished she could have it. Pretty soon, she would be grown up like me. Life would not be simple anymore. She sure wouldn't get to sit in a tree and be an angel eating a hot dog.

CHAPTER 13

"Mama! Jesse! Mama! Jesse!" The twins wanted the door open and fast. "Mamajessemamajesse!"

"What do ya'll want?" I asked. I swear when I grow up I may not even have kids.

"Dowis Way wants down," Roy Dean said.

"Tell her I'll be there in a minute."

I got Blanky, Doris Ray's raggedy old baby blanket, and carried it outside to the tree.

I looked up at Doris Ray. I could see her real good, being that most of the leaves were gone. She'd climbed to a higher branch and sat scared to death, her arms wrapped around the center trunk.

"I want down. Get me down, Jesse," she whined.

"You *said* you wanted to live up there," I reminded her. "Here's Blanky, so you can spend the night." I grinned up at her. I should have stopped teasing her, helped her get down. Instead I tossed Blanky high into the skeleton tree toward Doris Ray's angel wings. But I missed. Finally I hit a limb a little farther than an arm's length from her. She reached out, but her fingers were still about an inch away. Gripping the trunk with one hand, she stretched again, barely touching the edge of Blanky. This time she let out a shriek.

The next thing I knew, her halo slipped and fell through the air, the tinsel streaming in circles like a kite tail.

"You just about made me fall," Doris Ray wailed. "I'm telling Mama, and I'm gonna tell her about some other stuff, too."

"Mama's taking a shower. She's not even around to tell," I said. "What's the matter, Miss Queen Angel, can't you fly down?"

Doris Ray hollered, "Ma-a-a-ma!" Then she asked, "Where's Daddy?"

"Out back under his truck. He can't hear you, crybaby," I said.

She stuck her tongue out, then hollered anyway. "Da-a-a-ddy, Da-a-a-ddy."

"I'm going in. Sweet dreams," I told her. "There's supposed to be a full moon tonight, so it won't get *that* dark."

Doris Ray hates the dark. She screamed even louder.

I turned around real quick, too quick, because I caught my shoe on the roots under the tree and lost my balance.

"Now look what you made me do," I yelled up at her.

A thin red stream dribbled from my palm to my wrist where I'd tried to catch myself. "I've gotta go in and wash this off."

Doris Ray stopped crying and squinted down at me. "Let me see," she said. My sister gets a kick out of seeing someone else bleeding, but if it's her *own* blood, she thinks she's dying.

I held my hand as high as I could, but her interest didn't hold long. "*Get me down!*" she demanded, turning the volume way up.

"See you in the morning!" I teased, not looking back. As the screen door slammed, Doris Ray cranked up. I was going to let her cry just long enough to clean up my hand, then I was going to go back and get her, and the joke would be over.

While I watched the hydrogen peroxide bubble on my cut, turning it pink, the boys came banging at the door again. Only this time they sounded different, more in a panic, like the time Jimmy poked a stick at the wasp's nest in the honeysuckle.

I ran to the door. The boys looked frantic.

"Dowis Way!" Roy Dean screamed. "She fell out the twee!"

I raced outside. "Run get Mama," I cried to Jimmy. "And Roy Dean, go 'round back and get Daddy. He's under his truck."

I saw Doris Ray in a white heap at the base of the cottonwood, her face in the dirt and her wings all bent and crooked. When I got next to her, I saw a trickle of blood running from her nose, but there was a bigger puddle seeping out from under her forehead.

Shaking, I lifted her little hand. It felt cold and limp. She wasn't moving at all.

"Doris Ray!" Mama screeched.

I looked behind me. Mama ran toward us, barefoot, her bathrobe flying behind her. Her eyes had the same look they did the night William III got so sick.

Daddy came running around the corner, all greasy and black with oil.

"Call an ambulance!" Mama said, but Daddy said it'd take too long because they're all volunteers around here.

"I'm taking her myself," he said.

I licked my finger and was going to hold it up to Doris Ray's mouth to make sure she was still breathing, but Daddy swooped her up and carried her around back. Mama and me and the boys ran behind him.

"You watch the twins, Jesse." Daddy climbed into the car and handed Mama the keys.

They sped out of the yard and my legs and arms went weak. I collapsed in the gravel.

"Is Dowis Way gonna be like Goldie?" came a little voice from behind me. Goldie was Roy Dean's goldfish we buried in the garden last summer.

Dear God, please don't let her be, I thought, standing up. I picked up Roy Dean even though he's way too big. His feet knocked me in the shins the whole way. "Come on, Jimmy," I said. "You'll have to walk, I can only carry one at a time."

We went inside and I wrapped up in the afghan on the couch. I shouldn't have been cold, but I was shivering.

I knew everything that would happen. We'd have to

pack up all Doris Ray's stuff. Mama would be crying real quiet while she folded her clothes and I'd be patting her on the back. We'd have to put everything in boxes. After a few months we'd haul them out of the closet, and we'd get rid of them forever. Pretty soon, just like with William III, there wouldn't be a trace of Doris Ray anywhere.

I'd freeze her up inside of me and promise myself never to say her name again.

A few minutes later, the phone rang. My legs went weak again, and my stomach felt like it was on an elevator. I expected to hear Mama say, "She's gone," like she did that other morning.

On the fourth ring, I picked it up and said hello.

"Jesse?" the voice said.

I tried to say something besides uh-huh, but I couldn't. Nothing came out except a bunch of crying.

"Jesse? This is Mrs. Noble. What's the matter, dear?"

I started to talk, but only a scratchy noise came out like a wire pad scraping a skillet.

"Jesse, are you all right?" she was saying. "Tell me what's wrong."

Then I said it. "Mrs. Noble, I killed—her. I killed Doris Ray just like I killed my—like when I killed—" I choked into tears again.

Mrs. Noble asked me if my parents were home, and I managed to say no. By this time, the twins were bawling, too.

Mrs. Noble said she knew the trailer court where we lived and that she was coming over. She told me to stand out front so she'd know which trailer.

I hung up the phone and picked up an orange peel that someone had left on the couch. My mouth was all dry and I could hardly move, like I was walking through deep water. I just wanted to sink or at least hide in the dark in the closet. But I couldn't on account of the boys and Mrs. Noble coming, so I put on my jacket, set the boys in front of cartoons on the television and went on outside.

The tree was a big black spider in the sky. Blanky still hung from a limb way up high, and the wind whipped it back and forth. It looked like a ghost. I picked up Doris Ray's broken halo and wrapped the Christmas tinsel around it again. I wished Roxanne was home, but she was at work.

Just then, Mrs. Noble drove up in a Jeep. "Hi, Jesse," she said, getting out. "What have you got there?"

I looked at the halo in my hands and started to cry again.

Mrs. Noble put her arm around me and we walked up to the front door.

"Now, dear, are you all right? What's all this about your killing someone?" she asked.

Suddenly the phone rang. I felt my stomach take another dive. Shaking, I picked up the receiver. It was Mama. She wanted to know if the boys were doing okay and I said yes, holding my breath. Then she told me Doris Ray had been taken from Dr. Harris's to the hospital in Corn Valley. A surgeon had set her leg.

"You mean she's not dead?" I whispered.

Mama said she was completely alive. Didn't I know that? She'd been knocked out for a few minutes, but she came to before they even got out of the trailer park. Had a cut on her head that took some stitches. She'd gotten a mild concussion, too, but she was going to be fine. Especially since she had a remote control in her room.

"She wanted Blanky," Mama told me, "but Daddy bought her a whale in the hospital gift shop and she's doing okay. All the nurses are making a fuss over her like she's some kind of beauty queen."

"Are y'all coming home pretty soon?" I asked.

"Your Daddy and I want to spend the night up here, Jesse. Would you be afraid to stay by yourself with the boys?"

"No, I'm not afraid, and anyway Roxanne'll be right next door," I said. "Mrs. Noble has stopped by, too. Everything is fine." Mama told me to be sure to offer Mrs. Noble some hot tea and gingersnaps and that she'd call later.

"You look better, Jesse," Mrs. Noble said when I got off the phone. I told her that when she'd called earlier I was out of my mind worrying about Doris Ray. I wasn't thinking right and probably said something dumb.

Just like at school, Mrs. Noble wasn't going to let me off that easy. "What were you saying about killing someone, Jesse?"

"Oh, that," I said, feeling real embarrassed. "When Doris Ray fell out of the tree, I'd been kind of teasing her and, well, it seemed like my fault at first."

"I thought you were talking about someone else, too," she said.

I shook my head. "I was thinking about my brother. A long time ago, he got sick and died." Mrs. Noble's blue blouse all of a sudden seemed to swim in front of me like a big piece of ocean water. I wiped my eyes with my sleeve.

"I'm sorry, dear," she said.

"Yeah," I answered. "Would you care for some cookies and a cup of tea?"

Mrs. Noble said the tea sounded nice. A few minutes later, while she dipped the tea bag in and out of her cup, she talked to me.

"Do you remember my telling the class about *The Aeneid*, Jesse?"

"I guess," I answered, wondering what she was getting at.

"When the city of Troy burned, Aeneas had to leave and start over. He had to learn that he couldn't rebuild the old one. I guess we have to leave our old hurts behind, don't we?"

I nodded, but I doubted she understood.

Thankfully, she changed the subject. "I was calling you earlier, Jesse, to tell you about a meeting of the news staff in Mr. Huber's office on Monday morning. Try to come if you can."

I said I'd be there and that I appreciated it that she came by. After she left, I made the boys some tomato soup and toast and we all sat in front of the TV and ate dinner.

Later that night, Mama called again. "I've phoned Roxanne at the café to ask her to keep an eye on you. I told her about Doris Ray, and she offered to take you and the boys up to the hospital tomorrow afternoon. She'll take you to church first, of course."

"Do we have to go to church since you and Daddy aren't here?" I asked.

"Roxanne said she'd really like to go, that she'd been meaning to anyway." Mama sounded pleased and I decided not to argue. Maybe she'd quit griping about Roxanne after this.

After the boys went to bed, I cleaned the kitchen and picked up the toys in the living room. Around ten o'clock, Roxanne knocked on the door.

She came in and hugged me and said she'd spend the night if I needed her to. But I said no. I'm thirteen and it's about time I handled things without a grown-up around.

"Are you sure you want to go to church?" I asked. "I really don't mind missing it for once."

"I told your Mama I'd take y'all, and I'm going to," she said. As usual, there wasn't any changing her mind.

"Wear something churchlike!" I said as she left to go home. I wasn't sure how she'd fit in at Community Shepherd.

"Don't worry." She grinned, waving as she walked across our yard to hers.

I didn't feel very confident, but I was real tired and when I lay down on the couch, I fell right to sleep and didn't wake up until the next morning.

CHAPTER 14

"Are you wearing that?" I couldn't believe my eyes. Roxanne stood at the door in a blue suede mini-skirt, black fishnet hose, and a tight red sweater.

"It's the closest thing I have to church clothes," she said. "Do I look like a stained-glass window?"

"Not exactly. At least not one at our church."

"Jesse, you are so-o-o serious. I've got my coat in the car, if that's what's bothering you."

It didn't matter to her one bit that those fake furs went out of style years ago or that hers was almost two sizes too big. She said the feeling she got when she wore it was the important thing.

When we got to the church, Roxanne stood in the parking lot bundling up, wrapping her coat around herself real good.

"How do I look?" she asked.

"You look pwetty," Roy Dean told her.

I said she looked fine even though in March nobody needs a real heavy coat.

"I'm so nervous," Roxanne whispered as we walked across the parking lot. "It's been a long time since I've been in a church."

A few people said hello to us and stared at Roxanne as we got nearer the doors.

Roxanne stopped. "I changed my mind," she said.

"Okay," I told her. "Let's go on to the hospital."

We turned back toward the car and she stopped again. "No, we're staying. We're here, now." Roxanne tiptoed toward the church steps trying to keep her heels from sticking in the gravel.

Once we got inside the entryway of the sanctuary, we could hear the piano already playing. Roxanne stopped to look at the missionary pictures pinned on the bulletin board. She was squeezing her arms real tight in front of her like she was freezing.

"Are you sick or something?" I asked.

She thought a few seconds. "I'm all right. Let's go sit down."

Mrs. Cordell had already started playing "Onward Christian Soldiers" for the choir to march in. Suddenly Jimmy dug his heels into the linoleum and Roy Dean sat down on the floor.

"You two get up this instant," I hissed. Just at that moment the Harrises walked in.

I was about to suggest we leave, but before I had a chance to say anything, Roxanne'd scooted behind the artificial palm that stands next to the sanctuary doors.

"We're running late," Dr. Harris mumbled.

"Yeah, us too," I said, glancing at Roxanne, who was kind of crouching behind some leaves. She looked like she was scared to death, but as the Harrises started down the aisle of the church to find a seat, she stepped out.

"What in the world is wrong with you?" I asked her. "Are we going in or not?" Roxanne stared right through me.

"It's him," she said, her eyes watering up.

"Who?" I asked.

"It's *him* . . . you know . . . ," she repeated.

Then it dawned on me. "The baby?" I whispered, not believing what I was hearing.

She bit her bottom lip and nodded.

"You're . . . Frankenstein's mother?" My mouth suddenly went dry, and my stomach took a dive just like it did when I thought I'd killed Doris Ray.

"Come on," she said. Roxanne held her head high and marched into church. I followed her with the boys. The Harrises were sitting near the front in an empty pew and Roxanne went right toward them. About a hundred eyes drilled into us, mostly into Roxanne in her coat and skinny fishnet ankles and silver spike heels.

She went straight to where the Harrises sat and sank down right next to Frankenstein, practically touching him. I followed next, then the boys. And when the music ended, Roxanne looked at me and smiled.

"Good morning, folks-s-s . . . and visitors-s-s." Pastor Cordell looked straight at Roxanne. Running his hand over the bald strip on the middle of his head, he announced, "I'm sure glad to see *Jess*-see sitting up here with her brother-s-s and her guest this morning." I looked at Roxanne, but she was a million miles away.

"We got a call last night about our little angel *Do*-ris *Ra*-ay who is in the *hos-spit-al* on this Lord's day." Pastor Cordell can make one word last as long as a sentence.

"She fell out of a *tree-ee* last evening and we'll all want to re-*mem*-ber her in our *pray*-ers." Mrs. Cordell took that as her cue and began playing "Amazing Grace."

Roxanne was busy staring at Frankenstein's hand resting on the seat beside her. During the prayer, which was partly for Doris Ray's broken leg and partly for Mrs. Caruthers's kidney stone, I glanced at her again. She had her head down and she was smiling. I looked at Frankenstein, and my insides felt like Jell-O.

For the whole sermon Roxanne hardly moved except to breathe, and every once in a while to dab at the sweat on her forehead. Her furry shoulder was only about two inches from Frankenstein's; her fingers almost touched his.

Right near the end of the service, Roxanne stood up. Tears streamed down her face, which was all red from the heat. People all around craned their necks to watch as she inched her way past me and the boys. When she got to the end of the pew, she stopped a second and looked toward Frankenstein, then she ran down the aisle—not toward the front where Pastor Cordell held out his arms like Jesus, but straight toward the clock in the back and on out the doors.

A few minutes later, when the service was over, Dr.

Harris leaned toward me and asked, "Is your friend all right?"

I nodded. "She's just missing her family, I think. They live somewhere else."

"At the zoo?" Frankenstein said.

His mother frowned. "That's not nice, Franklin. Now, you go on outside." She touched my arm. "I'm sorry, Jesse. Franklin doesn't always say the right thing."

I wanted to say, "No joke," but instead I just nodded. "Excuse me, but we've got to go. We're on our way to the hospital to see Doris Ray."

"Give her our love," Mrs. Harris said. I told her I would and hurried outside. Jimmy and Roy Dean were wrestling on the grass in front of the church. Frankenstein was out there with them.

"Y'all get up," I yelled. The boys were getting filthy and Roy Dean had already torn a little hole in one knee of his good Sunday pants.

He pointed at Frankenstein. "He pulled me awound," he said, giggling.

"Can't you see they have their good clothes on?" I fired at Frankenstein.

"You mean *had* their good clothes on," he said, grinning.

"Where's Roxanne?" I asked Jimmy.

I looked toward the parking lot. The car was gone. *Now what,* I thought. It wouldn't be that easy to walk home with the boys, and I'd have to call the hospital and tell Mama we couldn't come. She'd think she was right about Roxanne all along—and maybe she was.

We'd only walked a few feet when she pulled up,

honking long and loud like she was at a drive-in restaurant or something. I frowned at her, but she was smiling real big and tapped the horn again just before she bent across the seat and pushed open the front door for me.

"Why are you honking?" I asked. People were watching us like we were crazy or something.

"Get in," she said, grinning. "Let's hit the road!" The boys climbed into the backseat where Roxanne's mouton coat was piled in a heap, and I got in the front.

"There's nothing like leaving town!" Roxanne said as we headed down the highway. "You boys ready to go see an angel?" She sounded bubbly and excited, like it was someone else bawling her eyes out just fifteen minutes before.

"We gonna see a angel?" Jimmy asked.

"You bet your booties, we are. A real live angel, a genuine fallen angel." Roxanne said "genu*ine*," like it was a kind of fancy wine. She winked at me and said to loosen up.

"Where'd you go?" She'd run out of church embarrassing me to death, she'd given me the shock of my life before that, and to make matters worse, she almost left us.

"Oh, I just ran down to the convenience store. Got some ginger ale and moon pies to celebrate."

"Celebrate what?" I grumbled.

"Know what song I'm playing?" she said, ignoring me.

"None. Your radio's broken."

"Wrong!" she answered. "It's 'Oh, what a beautiful morning; oh, what a beautiful day . . . ,' " she sang as she tapped the rhythm on the steering wheel with her long nails.

"Jesse, if you'll quit biting your nails and let 'em grow so you can tap out a song on the dashboard, I'll give you . . . my mouton coat!"

"Yeah, sure," I said, tucking my short, ragged nails into my fists. "Like you'd really part with your Snow Queen outfit."

She tilted her head back and laughed.

"Why are you in such a good mood, anyway? You couldn't wait to get out of church."

"I bet everybody in that place thought I was going to go up and repent my sinful life. And I was just going to get moon pies!"

I halfway smiled, but I was still aggravated about everything, especially about Frankenstein.

"How could that creep be your you-know-what? And how can you be so happy about it?" Even though the boys were too young to understand, I didn't want them to know what I was talking about.

"It was wonderful, Jesse. He's really cute."

"Are you sure we're talking about the same person?"

"The thing is, his hands are exactly like Johnny's. That plaster hand in my bedroom could be his. The fingers are long and kind of squared at the tips."

I knew the hand she was talking about. I'd looked at it plenty of times, but I'd never thought about it looking like Frankenstein's.

"It just about killed me at church that I couldn't reach out and touch those fingers," she said.

"Oh, brother. I can't believe my ears," I said.

"You're going to have to help me, Jesse. Remember what I told you? I still need to hug my baby. We've got to figure out a way." Roxanne's happy mood had suddenly turned.

"Why don't you just have some more kids? Get your mind off the one you lost."

The air felt heavy like it does before one of those big gully-washer rains. Roxanne just shook her head.

We drove on and neither one of us said a word for a long time. Even the boys, who usually never shut up on a trip, were quiet, looking out the windows at all the oil pumps in the bare fields. Sometimes you see them moving up and down like iron teeter-totters, but that day they were mostly dead still. I was glad when we finally saw the buildings of the city.

CHAPTER 15

Once we reached the city, hardly any time passed at all before we got to the hospital and rode the elevator up to the seventh floor to Doris Ray's room. When we got there, Mama and Daddy were sitting in orange vinyl chairs next to her bed, and Doris Ray was ruling the world—or at least the hospital room.

She was propped up like the Queen of Sheba, surrounded by balloons and toys and books. The very first thing she said when we walked through the door was, "Hi, Jesse, did you bring me anything?"

I swear, falling out of a tree didn't change her one bit.

"We bwought us," Roy Dean told her.

"Yeah," I said. "I brought your brothers."

"Je-e-e-sse!" Doris Ray whined. "I meant, did you bring a present?" She stuck her bottom lip out and frowned.

Mama said, "Doris Ray, now you hush. Your sister and brothers have come all this way to see you."

Roxanne stood in the doorway in her mouton coat, and Mama added, "And Roxanne came, too. Take your coat off, Roxanne. Doris Ray's been waiting all day for you all to get here."

Roxanne peeled off her fur and stuffed it in the tiny closet across from Doris Ray's bed.

"*Wow!* You look beautiful!" Doris Ray said when she saw Roxanne's blue suede miniskirt.

"Where'd you get *them*?" Doris Ray pointed at the floor.

"What? My outfit?"

"No," Doris Ray said, "your shoes."

"These old things?" Roxanne answered, taking off her silver heels. "Thrift Town. I put the glitter on myself, though."

"They look like the Blue Fairy's shoes in *Pinocchio*."

"Tell you what, baby. Soon as you get that old cast off, you can have them."

Doris Ray just about wet her pants. "Really?" she squealed. I swear she doesn't even think. Those shoes wouldn't fit her for ten years.

"I brought you something else, too." Roxanne dug around in her purse and pulled out a little cellophane package.

"What is it?" Doris Ray sat up straight in bed trying to see. "Let me see, let me see!" she shrieked.

"Your very own solar system, so you don't have to sleep in trees to see the stars." Roxanne reached into the package and pulled out a tiny white star about the size of Doris Ray's littlest toenail.

"I ordered them from one of those gadget catalogs. I planned to put them in my bedroom if I ever stayed anywhere long enough."

"You should keep them," I said. "I'll help you put them up in your own bedroom."

"No, Doris Ray'll be around a lot longer than I will," she said. "The ad claimed there's at least fifteen hundred glow-in-the-dark stars and planets per bag. Stick 'em on the ceiling and walls in your bedroom and, come night, you'll be sleeping right under the Milky Way!"

"Oo-o-o, Jesse, will you put them up when we get home?" Doris Ray couldn't wait.

I said I guessed so. I mean, what choice did I have with Doris Ray in a cast and all?

"So," Roxanne started up, "how in the world did you manage to fall out of that old tree?"

Here it comes, I thought. *The reason I'll be grounded for the rest of my life*.

"Cause I was going to play a trick on Jesse," Doris Ray said. "Cause I was pretending I was a squirrel and I was going to throw a little piece of bark down and hit her on the head, but I slipped accidentally."

I couldn't believe what Doris Ray was saying. That wasn't how it happened at all.

"I thought you were an angel," Mama said. "You were wearing your wings and everything."

"I *was* an angel at first. Then I was a squirrel. Angels can turn into whatever they want to. I wanted Jesse to leave me alone. I thought she was going to make me come down and I wanted to stay up there."

Doris Ray knew good and well that wasn't how it happened, but she wasn't going to budge. She was determined to help me out. I got down next to her bed and gave her a little hug.

When the doctor came by, he said Doris Ray could go on home. She threw a fit, begging to ride with me and Roxanne. I didn't really want her to, but what could I say? So Mama and Daddy took the boys in the car with them, and we took Doris Ray with us. Practically as soon as she got in the car, she fell asleep, and for a lot of miles Roxanne and I didn't say too much.

In my mind I made a list of why I should help Roxanne figure out a way to get her hug. Pros and Cons.

On the Pro side:

1. Roxanne's my best friend.

On the Con side:

1. Franklin Harris is a jerk.
2. He's never done or said one nice thing to me.
3. Being around him more than working on the paper will ruin my reputation.
4. He'll probably hurt Roxanne's feelings.
5. He doesn't deserve a hug from anybody.

I was still deciding on things to add when Roxanne interrupted my thoughts.

"You know when you asked me why I didn't have more kids?"

"Yes."

"Well, I can't have any more."

"You're not too old," I told her. "My aunt had a baby when she was forty!"

"It's not that. I almost had another baby. With Robert. I got pregnant, but we got in a fight, not just an argument. Things happened. I miscarried and had to have a hysterectomy after that."

"You had to have a what?"

"Had to have my plumbing taken out. You know, all the stuff that lets you have babies. I probably didn't want any more anyway."

I didn't know what to say, so I told her a story Mama'd told me.

"When my mother was a little girl, her mother had a miscarriage. Mama said Grandma made a little coffin out of an Ivory Soap box and buried it under the apple tree. She said Grandma used to stand at her kitchen window washing dishes and staring at that tree for hours on end. Mama said women never forget their babies even if they don't get born."

"Well, that's true. Mine wasn't any bigger than the moon out there."

I looked out the window where it was already dark. There was only a tiny piece of the moon the size of a scrap of lemon rind.

"Close one eye," Roxanne said. "Now cover the moon up with your finger. See? It's not any bigger'n your little pinkie."

"You had a baby that small?" I tried to picture it—a baby that would fit in a matchbox.

"When you have one that early, you really can't see it

that good. It's like starting your period, only with more bleeding. I hurt real bad, like cramps only a thousand times worse. I'm sure you know what cramps feel like."

I nodded in the dark even though I was probably the only eighth-grade girl in Eli Whitney, in Texas even, who hadn't started yet.

"Anyway," Roxanne said, "even if your baby is no bigger than an idea, you can't forget it. For weeks you have this dream growing inside you. You think about it all the time, even at the grocery store when you're picking out frozen vegetables. Pretty soon, you're thinking about names. You're taking big pink vitamins and eating eggs for breakfast and drinking milk instead of having Chee-tos and Coke. Then all of a sudden, everything's gone."

Roxanne rolled the window down and let the cool air blow in, whipping her hair outside.

"Robert was bad. Don't ever let a man—anyone—slap you around, Jesse."

I said I wouldn't, and I meant it. Roxanne told me stuff no one else ever had. To her, I wasn't just a kid, I was somebody, really somebody.

I don't know if it was because of what she told me or that it was so dark or that Doris Ray was snoring like a kitten in the backseat, but I told Roxanne all about William III. For the first time ever, I admitted what I'd never been able to say aloud. I told her how I wouldn't pray for him at dinner like Mama told me to. How I felt bad for so long. How at his funeral when we sang "Itsy Bitsy Spider," I couldn't even cry. Then I told her about

Doris Ray, how I hadn't helped her out of the tree when she wanted down.

On that long dark highway with Roxanne beside me, I bawled my heart out. And she patted me on the leg and said it was all right.

CHAPTER 16

It was like getting dressed in a planetarium the next morning. But that's not what made me late to the meeting in Mr. Huber's office.

First, Doris Ray had to have some cocoa. Then she had to have some pretzels, even though it was only six o'clock in the morning. After that, all her animals had to be lined up around her and it took ten minutes to find Pat, her stuffed parrot. Finally, when everything was all set, she had to go to the bathroom, which is not that easy with a cast.

"I'm going to be late for school," I told her. I noticed it was six-thirty and the meeting with Mrs. Noble and Mr. Huber was supposed to be at seven-fifteen.

"Did you hear me? I'm going to be late!"

"Tough titty," she said.

"What? Where did you learn that?" I shot back. Mama would've washed my mouth out.

"You said it one time."

"I did not."

"Did too," she whined.

"Did not. But you better not go around saying that in front of Mama unless you like the taste of soap," I warned her as I pulled off my nightgown.

That's when I saw it. A stain the color of the rust around the faucet outside.

"What's that?" Doris Ray wanted to know.

"Nothing," I said, even though I felt all weak and shaky inside.

"Go on back to sleep," I snapped.

"How'd you cut yourself . . . there?"

"None of your big fat business."

"Maaa-maaa," Doris Ray hollered. "Jesse said none of my big fa-a-a-at business."

"Hush," I said. At this rate, I knew I'd be lucky if I even made it to school, much less to the early meeting.

Mama met me at our bedroom door.

"Jesse cut herself and bleeded on her nightgown," Doris Ray announced.

I thought I'd just die right there. I mean, I have no privacy. Mama looked at me like I was broken out in hives or something, then said for me to get the stuff I needed out from under the sink in the bathroom.

"I'm supposed to be at school early," I said, heading down the hall, "and Doris Ray won't leave me alone."

For once Mama was on my side. She told Doris Ray to settle down and let me get ready in peace. Then she left and came back in a few minutes with a cup of hot tea, full of sugar and milk the way I like it.

The one day I'd waited for for so long had finally happened. And nothing was different, not one thing. I looked in the mirror to see if I had changed, but I hadn't. All the freckles were still there. The same plain green eyes without moon pools stared back at me. I pulled up my sweater. My bra still wrinkled in all the places where it's not supposed to.

I looked at my watch, gulped down the last swallow of my tea, the thick sugary part, and headed out the door. By the time I got to school, things had already gotten started without me. There was a note taped to Mrs. Noble's door: "Jesse, go to Mr. Huber's office ASAP."

I ran down the empty hall; it was still too early for kids to be coming in. Mr. Huber's door was open just far enough for me to see his prize rattlesnake, which sits stuffed and coiled on the corner of his desk. I peeked inside and saw Debbie, Mrs. Noble, and Frankenstein sitting on folding chairs. Mr. Huber was rolling his ballpoint pen between his hands like he was trying to start a fire.

He cleared his throat and looked at his watch, and Mrs. Noble motioned for me to sit down next to her.

"As I was about to say, before Jesse came in," he said, stopping to clear his throat again, "I'm surprisingly rather pleased with this newspaper venture." Mrs. Noble looked at me and raised her eyebrows in an it's-not-what-I-expected-either look.

Mr. Huber set down his pen and picked up his tomahawk paperweight. "I'm proud of promoting student creativity and excellence here at Eli Whitney," he went on. I couldn't believe my ears. This was the same man who had threatened to rip up all of our newspapers when we'd printed an article about teachers who came into class smelling like cigarette smoke.

"And you, Franklin, have made our school proud," Mr. Huber added, smiling so big his fillings showed.

Frankenstein squirmed in his chair like he'd sat on a prickly pear.

Mr. Huber tapped the tomahawk on his palm for emphasis. "I saw the newspaper this week before it went to press and I thought your cartoon was outstanding. I'm sending copies not only to the members of the school board, but also to the sheriff, the mayor and the editor of *The Daily Star*. I think it's a good idea for a big city newspaper as well as our own community leaders to recognize the outstanding work of young people, work that promotes the mission of our school in our community and shows the larger world surrounding us what we're about."

Frankenstein squirmed some more. I figured he was more used to being chewed out than praised and he was really uncomfortable.

This is how it happened. One morning right before our news deadline, we'd had a huge argument. Frankenstein brought in his latest cartoon, and when I saw it I said, "You've got to be kidding." There was Mr. Huber sitting in an outhouse with his pants wadded around his feet. He wore radio headphones and was reading an issue of *Education Gazette*. Beyond the outhouse was our school. It had arms and legs and was running like it was about to lose a race. The school bell on top of the building was ringing and the caption read, "Will Eli Whitney be tardy for the future?"

"You can't have the principal sitting on a toilet," we'd all told Frankenstein. "Your point may be well taken," Mrs. Noble had said, "but your method is in error."

Frankenstein had exploded. "Nobody understands me! You're all backward, just like this school!" He'd stomped out of the room with his cartoon and we'd thought he might even quit.

Instead he'd showed up the next morning with a cartoon that wasn't anything like the other ones he'd drawn, which for the most part had been totally unacceptable. I mean you can't publish pictures of teachers mooning each other and get away with it. The cartoon Mr. Huber loved so much showed an exact likeness of himself standing with his arms spread out in a meadow of flowers. He had kids sitting and standing around his feet gazing up at him, and there was a kind of light like a giant halo shining around him. In the background there was an image of a cemetery. On the tombstones were carved different problems people associate with schools these days: guns, knives, lack of motivation, disrespect, and some more. Under the picture was the caption "Small rural schools deprive modern students."

Of course, the message was clear to Mr. Huber. Eli Whitney was a place you'd love to send your kids.

Even Mrs. Noble was suspicious of why Franklin had drawn such a thing, but at the last minute it had looked better than anything else we had. Debbie said Frankenstein definitely needed balance, but she said he had talent and we should be patient. With Frankenstein, patience doesn't come easy. Anyway, this drawing made Mr. Huber look like a saint, and he loved it.

"You kids may get on to class now. The paper will be delivered to our community friends the second it arrives. You're the kind of students who represent our school well." He stood and gave the school fight gesture, a few short chops into the air.

On the way out the door, Frankenstein said, "I almost told Mr. Huber where he can put his ignorant tomahawk chop. This whole school's a racist prison." He pushed by Debbie and me and headed down the hall.

The rest of the day was fairly quiet, but when I got home there was another surprise.

CHAPTER 17

I'd barely gotten in the door when Mama called me into the kitchen. "Roxanne's been over," she said, smiling. "She wants you to come by her place."

"Can I?" I asked.

She said I could and that I didn't have to take Doris Ray, either. I went right over.

At the porch I heard the radio playing real loud. Roxanne came to the door, grinning and wearing blue jeans, a green sequined T-shirt, and a New Year's Eve party hat. She'd strung crepe paper all over the place and I could smell popcorn.

"Come on in!" she said, pulling me across the doorway. "Cover your eyes!"

"What's going on?" I figured she must've gotten that twenty-cent raise she'd been wanting.

"Don't peek!" she warned. I heard her walk toward

the kitchen, then come back into the living room. "Okay," she announced, "open!"

She stood in front of me with a cake covered in pink icing. "Congratulations!" she said.

"For what?"

"I stopped by to see Doris Ray this morning and your mother told me it was a special day for you."

"I didn't know people celebrated stuff like this," I said, feeling really embarrassed.

"Well, some people do. As a matter of fact, I'm celebrating two things. You . . . and Mr. Arthur's party." She cut us both a piece of cake and handed one to me.

"What party?" I asked. "Have I missed something here?"

"I figured out a way to hug Franklin and do something nice for Mr. Arthur at the same time." She talked as she peeled the icing off her cake and put it in a little pile.

"We'll have a big going-away party at the wax museum. We'll put posters around the whole town. I'll put some up at the café, and you get your friend to put some up at the beauty shop. It'll be a dance, and I'll dance with Mr. Arthur and some of the guys I know from the café and maybe some of the boys from your school. Then I'll dance with Franklin."

Roxanne was talking so fast and was so excited, I hated to interrupt her, but I did. "He'd never show up. For one thing he got kicked out of the museum when Elma caught him trying to put a nose ring on Queen Elizabeth. Forget it, Roxanne."

"He'll come, Jesse. If a good friend asks him to, he'll do it."

"A good friend?" The word *friend* would be foreign to Frankenstein.

"Yeah, Jesse. You. You'll invite him and—"

"Whoa!" I said. "Hold it. I'd rather call up Jack the Ripper and invite him. Come on, Roxanne. We've never said two decent words to each other. And I'm not particularly interested in starting now."

I watched her nibble at her icing like Doris Ray always does, licking it off the fork prongs one at a time.

"Do you always eat the icing by itself?"

"Always leave the best for last. That way you got something to look forward to. Even if it is just icing."

"Roxanne, don't get your hopes up. About Franklin . . . "

"Last night I lay awake thinking about how lucky I am," she said, her words tumbling out airy and quick like bubbles from one of those rings you blow into. "I was lying awake thinking when I got the idea about the party. I thought, this is the perfect idea! Hey, Jesse, you can invite some cute guys from school. Who do you want to dance with?"

"You make everything sound so simple. You assume life's going to turn out right and it usually doesn't. Besides, I can't dance," I said.

"You can't?" Roxanne acted like she'd heard me say I couldn't swallow or something. She jumped up and changed the radio station. "First, we'll do the pony."

"The pony? I thought we were talking about dancing." It sounded like something they do on those exercise videos we watch in gym class.

"It *is* a dance. Lord, Jesse, you don't know anything.

When I was your age we did the pony all night long. And the twist, even though it was out of style."

"And the horse or whatever you call it is in style?" I guessed it fit in the same category as mouton coats, out of date for everyone except her.

"Good things don't go out of style," she said, jumping around in a little gallop that did sort of look like a horse.

I sat down and watched her pony across the living room, into the kitchen, and back again. Finally the song was over and she stopped. "So. Do you think you could do that?" she asked.

"Sure," I said, thinking I wouldn't do it for a hundred dollars. "I don't even need to practice."

"What about slow dancing? You ever done that?"

I had, once. I shrugged. "I guess."

"And?" she waited. "Who'd you dance with? You never told me about a boyfriend." Roxanne had put on her glittery cat-eye glasses and she looked over the top of them at me.

"It wasn't a boyfriend. Just River Winston. Those glasses are weird."

"Did you say Reever or River? Talk about odd," she said.

"River. Like the Colorado. Every girl in the whole school had a crush on him last year. He was a freshman."

"He must've seen those moon pools in your eyes!" Roxanne grinned at me.

"He just asked me to dance at this school party. Probably it was a dare," I said.

"Or maybe he liked you, Jesse."

"I don't know why he asked me. Nobody else did either. It was just one time, though."

I didn't tell her that after I danced with River I didn't wash my shoulder for a week. Right where he'd bent down and touched his lips at the edge of the neck of my dress.

"Well, there's nothing to slow dancing," Roxanne said, grabbing a pillow off the couch and hugging it to her. "If you like him and he likes you, there's nothing better."

"And if you don't like him, there's nothing worse," I joked.

"On the other hand, the right kind of music and a nice dance sometimes work miracles," Roxanne said back.

"I've told you before, I don't believe in miracles." I hoped she wasn't expecting one with Frankenstein.

CHAPTER 18

Of course I should have known something wasn't right about the cartoon Frankenstein had drawn of Mr. Huber. Nothing could be that easy—not with Frankenstein, anyway. Two days later, when the paper came back from the printer, we really had a problem.

The Icon has to be taken to Corn Valley to be typeset and printed on account of Ida doesn't have its own newspaper. Mrs. Noble usually takes it, picks it up, and brings it back to the school. But this time Frankenstein volunteered to help. His father was going to Corn Valley anyway and he'd just ride along. Mrs. Noble agreed, and we all thought that Frankenstein's outburst, when he'd called the school a "racist prison," was just one of his temper tantrums and he was already over it.

On Friday Frankenstein came in with the papers, printed and tied together in a neat bundle. He had removed the special copies that Mr. Huber wanted to give away and put each one in a big envelope with the person's name printed on the front: for example, Ken Ashton, Mayor. Mr. Huber was real impressed and immediately sent his secretary to put the copies in the mail. Because he was so busy, he didn't take time to look at any of them, which isn't that unusual. Even Mrs. Noble usually just picks up the papers and delivers them without checking them over. This time that was a big mistake.

The papers were handed out throughout the school during second period, and it took only a few seconds for the uproar to begin. On the second page where Mr. Huber was supposed to be standing with a halo of light was Frankenstein's other drawing—Mr. Huber sitting on the toilet.

A loud whistle interrupted every classroom in the school. Then came Mr. Huber's voice. "This is your principal speaking. I have an emergency announcement. All teachers are to collect each copy of the school newspaper immediately. I repeat, every copy of *The Icon* is to be picked up *now*!" Smoke was practically coming out of the speaker box in the corner of the ceiling.

A few minutes later, a pink pass came from the office. It had my name on it. Coach Parnell, my history teacher, told me to go to the office.

Frankenstein, Debbie, and Mrs. Noble were all there. Mr. Huber, his face as red as rhubarb, was pacing behind his desk. He was swinging his tomahawk in the air and making a kind of steaming sound like when the car radiator overheats. Finally, he stopped walking and faced us.

I thought he was about to speak, but that hissing sound kept coming out of his throat. He shook his head real hard and started pacing again.

He coughed. "Fortunately the newspapers for our community leaders have not been delivered yet," he said finally. "I shudder to think . . . " He stopped in the middle of the sentence and slammed his hand on his desk.

Mrs. Noble spoke up. "Honestly, Mr. Huber, I am just as shocked as you are. I'm sorry."

Mr. Huber's voice came out in little spurts. "Sorry . . . isn't . . . good . . . enough. Who—who—who is responsible for this—this outrage?" he spluttered. Then he shook his head again. I looked over at Debbie and she stood up.

"Mr. Huber, I have a confession to make. I did it. I switched the cartoon at the last second. Nobody knew about it. I know this was grossly immature and selfish." A tear ran crookedly down Debbie's scarred cheek. I looked over at Frankenstein.

He sat with his elbows on his knees and his head down. The tops of his ears burned red.

"Debbie," Mrs. Noble began, "you know that's not true. That wasn't your drawing. Franklin, don't you have something to say?"

Debbie spoke up real quick. "I didn't say I drew it. But I put it in the paper. There's nothing wrong with drawing something like that, in private. Publishing it was a mistake. And I take full responsibility." She said it with such force that I almost believed her.

But she didn't fool Mrs. Noble. "Mr. Huber, I do not

believe this is Debbie's fault. Though I have no proof, I believe another individual is entirely responsible," she said, staring straight at the top of Frankenstein's bowed head.

"Young man," Mr. Huber boomed, "did you switch these cartoons?"

Frankenstein didn't make a sound.

"I'm speaking to you. I expect you to look at me." Mr. Huber was standing over Frankenstein, who finally shook his head no.

"Okay, then. Debbie has taken responsibility. She'll be the one who is punished," Mr. Huber said. "And there will be no more newspapers at Eli Whitney."

"Mr. Huber, please don't punish the whole student body," Mrs. Noble pleaded. She said she'd make sure nothing like this happened again, that we were just adolescents, learning. When she took off her glasses and dabbed at her eyes with her lace handkerchief, Mr. Huber's shoulders seemed to relax a little.

Debbie said she'd write the school a public apology, that she'd do anything to keep the paper.

Mr. Huber turned his back to us. "You'll agree to print the other cartoon. Debbie will receive one week of in-school suspension, starting immediately." She'd have to sit in a little cubicle in the gym foyer and do her work alone, thinking about her crime.

I couldn't take it. I looked over at Frankenstein again. "How can you let Debbie do this? You know you're responsible, you—" Debbie interrupted me.

"Mr. Huber, Jesse and I are best friends. She's just trying to help me. I know what I did and I'm ready to pay." She picked up her books and stood waiting at his desk.

Frankenstein and I were told to go on to class and not to say one word in the hallway. I felt sick about Debbie being sent to school jail, but one thing kept ringing through my head. She'd called me her best friend.

The following week everyone was talking about Debbie.

"Did she really know about that X-rated stuff in the paper?" some kids in my math class wanted to know.

"Of course not," I answered. "She's got more sense than that. If you really want to know what happened, ask Franklin Harris."

The crowd moved from me to Frankenstein's desk, surrounding him like a swarm of locusts. I heard him say that he wanted to be left alone, and when I looked back he'd put his head down on his desk and covered it with his jacket.

Debbie did exactly what she'd promised. She wrote a public apology, which was pinned to every bulletin board in the school. And she served her suspension, never saying a word to anyone. I still couldn't understand why she'd taken the blame—and for Franklin Harris, of all people.

A week later Debbie and I were back working on the paper before school. Thankfully, Frankenstein was absent because of an orthodontist appointment in Corn Valley. I asked her why she'd helped him.

"He's never done anything for you," I said.

"For one thing," Debbie answered, "having someone confess gave us a better chance of keeping the paper."

"Yeah, and it should have been Frankenstein."

"Jesse, you and I both know that was not going to happen. For another thing, I just decided to let this be my onion."

"Your onion? Not that it doesn't make sense or anything," I said.

"Remember?" she replied. "It's on our masthead. 'I only gave you an onion, nothing but a tiny little onion, that's all, that's all.'"

"Oh yeah, now it makes sense," I said sarcastically. I never had understood that onion bit on the top of our paper.

"Fyodor Dostoyevsky. It was in *The Brothers Karamazov*."

"You mean Theodore?" I asked.

"No, *Fee*-a-door. It's Russian."

Mrs. Noble, who had just walked to the door, popped her head in. "He also wrote *Crime and Punishment*. I don't remember anything about an onion in *Brothers*, though. A good crossword puzzle question."

Debbie explained. "There was this lady who did only one nice thing her whole life. She pulled a tiny onion out of her garden and gave it to a starving woman."

"That's nice? I don't even like onions."

Debbie continued. "Well, when the lady dies, she ends up in the lake of fire. God sends an angel to rescue her. The angel's got that same onion with her. She tells the lady to grab on to the green part and she'll pull her out of the fire. So the woman reaches out and when she does, everybody else in the lake grabs on to her because they want out, too. Well, she can't stand it. She starts kicking them away and pretty soon, the onion breaks. Nobody gets out."

"That doesn't sound very hopeful to me," I said.

"The onion, one small deed, could have had a lot of power—that is, if the woman hadn't been so selfish."

"So? I still don't get it."

"It's the newspaper that's important, and at this time in his life, Franklin just couldn't do the right thing. I had to help, or we'd all have gone under."

I didn't think it was fair for her to have suffered for a week, having to do her homework and eat lunch alone, but she said it really wasn't bad at all. "I kind of enjoyed it," she told me. "It's quiet down there. You can get a lot done and still have time to read a good book in your spare time. I just about finished *Moby Dick*."

While she was suspended, five kids said they might help with the paper. I guess they figured with the cartoon and Debbie getting in so much trouble, working on *The Icon* was really pretty cool.

CHAPTER 19

Even after Debbie took the rap for him, Frankenstein still caused problems, mostly by drawing cartoons that could never be put in a school newspaper. He usually showed up to work on the paper, but he was completely unpredictable and moody, not to mention totally ungrateful for what Debbie had done for him. Still, Roxanne's words echoed in my mind constantly: "Just one hug, it would last me a lifetime." I wanted to help make her dream come true, but most days it seemed like it would take a miracle.

One afternoon when we were staying after school to work on a deadline, a new person showed up to help. Harold Peterson's the shyest student in our class and the smartest next to Debbie. We were surprised he came, but we were glad to have the extra help, especially since he knows a lot about computers.

Things were going pretty well at first. No one was bothering us and we were actually getting some work done. Frankenstein was sitting in the corner drawing when Debbie remarked that she wished she'd been born with good coordination.

"I keep hitting *shift* instead of *enter*," she complained.

"I'm halfway coordinated," I said, "but I wish I'd been born rich. When we walk around in our house, it has to be single file."

Debbie laughed, then said, "What would you wish for, Harold?"

He shook his head and grinned.

"Franklin? How about you?"

I couldn't believe Debbie still spoke to Frankenstein after spending a week in detention, but she'd told me one day, "Jesse, I'd rather be known for being merciful than just."

"What book did you get that out of?" I'd wanted to know, but she'd just laughed and said it was something her mother used to say.

Anyway, I wasn't paying any attention to Frankenstein's wish until I heard him say something about the Cherokee. Then I turned my head because I remembered Roxanne saying she'd wanted his parents to tell him about his background.

"What'd you say?" I asked.

He frowned. "I said I wished I lived somewhere else. Not in a little town that smells like a feedlot."

"No, before that," I said. "Something about Cherokee."

"I should've been born a hundred and seventy-five years ago. I'd have been a Cherokee warrior," he said.

"Your ancestors are Native American?" Debbie asked.

He nodded. "My great-grandfather or great-grandmother, I think."

"You think?" Debbie questioned. "You should do some research in geneology. The library in Corn Valley has a huge section—"

"No thanks," Frankenstein interrupted.

"The Cherokees were the ones who made the first written Native American alphabet," Debbie continued.

"Sequoya," Frankenstein added, surprising everybody. "He's the one who figured it out."

"And weren't the Cherokees run out of their land and sent to Oklahoma?" Debbie asked.

"Around the late 1830s," he answered. "It was called 'the Trail of Tears.' In Cherokee language it was 'the trail where we cried.' They shouldn't have been forced out of their own land. I'd have fought if I'd have been there." I couldn't believe it. Franklin Harris was practically having a conversation.

Debbie looked excited.

"Do you think your parents would mind if I called them? I'd like to do a story, maybe on what they know about their heritage," she said.

"They wouldn't be much help," Frankenstein mumbled.

"Oh, sure they would. People like to talk about things like that. I'll just call them up and—"

"No!" Frankenstein shouted. "I said they wouldn't be any help and I meant it."

"I met them at the PTA spaghetti supper," Debbie argued. "They're real nice."

"How many times do I have to say it? No! They're not even my real parents. Like I said, I shouldn't even be living in this stupid hick town!" he shouted.

"And I shouldn't be living here, either," Debbie said, almost as loud as Frankenstein. "I should be living with both of my parents in a nice little house with a pet dog and a white picket fence. And I should have a perfect face."

"It's not the same." Frankenstein ran his hand through his hair. "Your parents didn't dump you."

"And yours didn't, either." I couldn't help myself.

"How would you know?" he shot back. "Did you see it in your crystal ball? Your tea leaves?"

"I just meant sometimes a mother loves her kid too much to keep it." I thought of that afternoon in the Laundromat and the pain on Roxanne's face when she told me her secret.

"Since when did you become the authority on mother-love?" Frankenstein snarled.

"Okay, you two," Debbie said, walking between us. "Let's drop the whole thing for now. We've got a paper to get out."

The room got real quiet, but the air was full of tension, like it gets when there's a tornado watch. Debbie and Harold started working on the layout again, and Frankenstein went back to his corner.

I sat at my desk thinking. Frankenstein's parents were crazy about him. You could watch them at church and tell that. His dad was always putting his arm around him.

And the way his mother looked at him, it was plain to see how much she loved him. My parents didn't pay half that much attention to me. So why the part about being dumped?

And why was he so proud of a Native American background that was probably so far back in his family history that it didn't even matter? I never thought about where my parents came from and couldn't care less. No matter how much I tried, I couldn't figure him out. It gave me a headache to try. Roxanne says life is mostly confusion. She says it takes a miracle for things to line up just right, and if they ever do, it usually just lasts a second, or even less.

"Jesse?" Debbie was calling me.

"What?"

"It's getting late. Are you finished with your article?" I looked down at my page, which was mostly blank.

"Not quite," I said. "I can't concentrate."

"Me either," Debbie answered. "It's time to quit." She started picking up her pages and filing them in folders. "By the way, I got a letter from my dad yesterday. When school's out, I'm flying to London to meet him."

Harold stopped working and stood up.

"Too bad you're gonna have to fly clear over the ocean, Deb," I said. "I'm planning an exciting time right here in Ida. I'll probably be standing in a hot kitchen helping Mama make watermelon pickles. Or if I'm lucky, maybe I'll get to shell some black-eyed peas."

"My summer's not going to be all fun," Debbie said. "I've got another surgery on my face scheduled in July."

"So, what are they gonna cut off this time?" Frankenstein walked up to us and stood near Debbie with a smirk on his face. "Or are they going to glue on some new parts?"

Harold, who hadn't said a word all afternoon, spoke up. "Hey, you owe her an apology."

"Make me," Frankenstein sneered.

Harold took his hands out of his pockets. His blond hair looked almost white next to his face, which was getting redder and redder.

"That's okay," Debbie cut in. "I'm used to teasing."

"No, it's not okay," Harold said. "He needs to learn some manners."

Debbie glanced at Harold with surprise and for the first time ever, I saw her blush.

"Who're you saying needs to learn manners?" Frankenstein growled. "Some people around here enjoy calling other people names." He glared straight at me.

This time, my face felt hot.

Harold put his hands back in his pockets and nervously walked closer to him. "We're talking about what you said to Debbie, right now. You still haven't apologized."

"I'm not going to either," Frankenstein said, crossing his arms on his chest.

Harold stepped toward him. "Go home. And don't come back," he said.

Frankenstein pushed over one of the desks that separated himself from Harold. I expected to see the two of them on the floor any minute, but just then Mrs. Noble walked in. She'd been in the teacher's workroom photocopying stuff until it was time to lock up.

She looked straight at Frankenstein. "Young man, what is going on here?"

"Nothing," he said. "I'm quitting." He grabbed his drawing tablet and pencils and stormed out the door.

In a few minutes, the rest of us left to go home, too. I figured my chances of getting Frankenstein to come to a party at the wax museum now were just about at minus zero. It seems when things get bad, they usually take a sudden turn for the worse.

CHAPTER 20

"Have you thought of a way to get Franklin to the party?" Roxanne asked me later.

She'd just changed clothes from work and was standing on her head to get her blood circulating real good.

"Not exactly," I answered. I told her what had happened, all the things he said, except for the part about being dumped.

Slowly she bent her knees, lowered them to the floor, and sat up. "So his parents did tell him about his Cherokee background." She sounded pleased. "I wanted Franklin to feel connected to a past."

"He's got the past down pretty good," I said. "It's the *now* that he's not handling very well."

"It takes a lot of courage to live in the present," Roxanne said with a sigh. "I feel sad about how he's treated Debbie. About quitting the paper, he'll get over being mad. He'll have to. By the way, Elma came in the café today."

She looked at me like I understood what she was talking about. When I didn't say anything, she added, "A place has come up for her daddy. She said we ought to have the party next Saturday."

"Next Saturday? That's only a little over a week away!" I couldn't think how everything would ever work out by then.

"Let's have a Hawaiian theme," she said. "I've got bunches of travel posters. And we'll make flowers out of tissue paper. We can have leis and pineapple punch and snacks."

I was feeling even more worried. "How're we going to pay for all this?" I wanted to know.

"I've been saving," Roxanne said. "It's covered. I want Mr. Arthur to have the best going away of his whole life, and I want to have the best memory in the whole world of my night with my son."

"Don't get your hopes up," I warned. But I knew I had to do something.

At school on the Monday before the party, I got an idea.

"Franklin," I said, "I know you're not on the paper anymore, but my friend Roxanne and I are planning a going-away party for Mr. Arthur. We were wondering if you'd come and do some sketches for us. You know, draw some of the people at the party, things like that."

"How much?" he asked.

"Oh, just a few. And only for an hour or two. Or not even that long." Just be there, I was thinking.

He said, "I meant, how much are you paying me?"

"Uh, well, we haven't quite worked that out. I thought maybe you'd just do it for Mr. Arthur, you know, sort of a going-away gift."

"Forget it," he said, turning on his heels and walking away.

That afternoon I didn't tell Roxanne how discouraged I felt, but I thought there was no way I would ever get Frankenstein to change his mind.

The days before the party went fast. On Friday, after school, Roxanne, Debbie and I planned to meet at the museum to decorate. I still hadn't figured out what to do, and I was running out of time.

Roxanne and I got to Mr. Arthur's at the same time as Debbie, whose aunt pulled up to let her out. Roxanne went straight up to her.

"Hi, I'm Roxanne. I've heard all about how brilliant you are from Jesse, here."

Debbie set her cardboard box of decorations on the sidewalk and shook Roxanne's hand, looking at the glittery decals Roxanne had pasted on her nails.

"I've heard about you, too. Jesse talks about you all the time. And, of course, you've been the topic of conversation at my aunt's beauty shop." Debbie grinned that crooked grin of hers.

"I can't wait to hear about that," Roxanne replied, grinning back at her. We picked up our stuff and headed around the side of the church to the museum's basement entrance.

"I told Elma we were coming and she said we could go

on in and get started," I said, leading Roxanne and Debbie down the steps to the door.

First we had to make about a million paper flowers. Roxanne had all colors of tissue paper and each piece had to be folded like a fan and tied with a pipe cleaner, and then we had to spread out the layers of paper to make the flower big and puffy. We spent two hours and still didn't have near enough, but Roxanne said it'd have to do and I agreed.

We hung the Hawaiian travel posters, and wherever there was a bare spot we taped up strips of crepe paper in all different colors. Next came the stars and moons, which we cut out of cardboard and covered in silver and gold glitter. Roxanne brought fishing line to hang them with so they'd look real natural. Debbie was standing on a ladder hanging a moon when she got an idea.

"We could paint faces on these moons, like the man in the moon," she said.

"Sorry, Deb," I said, "Roxanne doesn't believe in a man in the moon. She says it's a woman—holding a baby, to be exact."

"Really?" Debbie answered. "The Mayans had a myth that the moon was a goddess who gave women the gift of being able to come and go as they pleased. That's why sometimes only part of the moon shows, and one night every month it disappears completely."

"What is this kid, an encyclopedia?" Roxanne laughed.

I shook my head. "Just about. Let's get this galaxy up here so we can go home." After we finished hanging the stars and moons, I thought we were through for good, but Roxanne disagreed. She'd borrowed a bunch of strings of tiny white Christmas lights from the café, and her idea was to wrap them around the whole place. While we were working on those, she brought up the beauty shop gossip.

"So what do the town spies have to say about me? And make it something juicy!" she said to Debbie.

Debbie laughed. "Let's see. Well, Mrs. Rutherford said you're really a topless dancer. That you came to Ida to try to recruit girls for some of those fancy dance places in the city."

"Yeah, right," I said, looking down at my chest.

Roxanne snickered. "What else?"

"Miss Deever was getting her gray dyed the other day and she talked about how you came to church with Jesse. She said you almost got saved, but you headed the wrong direction at the last minute." Debbie giggled. "She said her son, the one who 'got Jesus on the radio' last summer, was praying with all his might for you, but it didn't work."

"Maybe he was tuned to the wrong station," Roxanne said. "I know Wilbert. He comes into the café for breakfast every morning and always leaves a dime and winks at me on his way out."

"Oh, and one lady says you walk around your house in the nude," Debbie added.

"Of course!" Roxanne said. "Don't all topless dancers do that?"

"Anyway, my aunt says all those women are just jealous that The Cowboy Café is so popular a place these days," Debbie continued.

"Shoot," I said, "that place has always been crowded, not just since Roxanne got here."

"I don't doubt it," Debbie said. Then she grinned. "It wouldn't surprise me if the men like it more these days, though. But let me tell you, Roxanne, you're not the only one who gets gossiped about. They talk about me—even when I'm in the room." Debbie bent down to pick up another string of lights. "I was cleaning combs the other day, and they were discussing me. Mrs. Owen, the mortician's wife, said her husband had some kind of putty stuff that might fill in some of the gaps on my face. She says it does wonders for dead people."

Roxanne stopped. "She said that? That old sorry excuse for a—"

"Oh, I get suggestions like that all the time," Debbie interrupted. "They want me to get all kinds of vitamin creams, fake eyebrows, the whole bit. They think if they can get me ready for the prom by the time I'm a senior, I'll be a success in life."

"You haven't had it easy, Debbie," Roxanne said. "I don't know how you've coped. And now, your teenage years, boys and all."

"It's okay, really it is," Debbie answered. "My father told me I had to reimagine my face. He took me to visit some of the Gothic cathedrals in Europe to help me."

I climbed down from the ladder I was standing on. "And?" I said.

"Fires used to destroy parts of the churches, and the people would just build on a brand-new design right onto the old part. They wouldn't tear the whole thing down and start over. They thought the old and new should be mixed together. It made it more interesting and beautiful."

I looked at Roxanne to see her reaction. She was thinking, gazing up to where the pipes made mazes on the ceiling.

"I like boys," Debbie added, "but I can't help it if they haven't learned to appreciate cathedrals!"

Roxanne laughed. "You've sure got it together, kid! Jesse, this is a girl who can take life and actually make some sense out of it. Stick around her!"

I said I would, but I wanted to know why she'd been studying the ceiling like it was a puzzle to be solved.

"I'm trying to figure out if we could hang the mermaid angel from these pipes over here," she answered. "I'd like to move it from the Lord's table to the dance floor."

Mr. Arthur's life-size mermaid was made from papier-mâché, except for the wings, which Mr. Arthur had made himself by gluing shiny gold feathers to a wire base covered with some kind of fabric. It hung from the ceiling pipes on long wires and it looked like it'd be a lot of trouble to move. Before I had a chance to complain though, Roxanne grabbed me by the shoulders.

"Jesse, run and ask Elma if it'd be all right to move her. Tell her we'll be real careful. I want her hanging over everybody tomorrow." She looked anxious, so I turned and started up the stairs even though I figured it would be a lot of trouble for nothing.

Elma was sitting on the floor in her living room. She was gluing dried kidney beans onto a big cardboard picture of a rooster. "When I get these beans painted, you won't even know what the thing's made of," Elma said.

"I saw one of these at the state fair in Dallas and ever since I've wanted one."

I said it was real pretty. Then I told her about Roxanne wanting to move the mermaid angel and how we promised to be careful.

"She's coming down anyway," Elma said. "We've sold most of this old junk to a dealer, but the nursing home administrator said they'd like to have her. I showed them a picture. They're gonna put her in the rec room where they play bingo."

I said thanks and went back down to the basement to tell Roxanne. "I didn't think she'd care," she said. She climbed up on the Lord's table and carefully untwisted the angel's wires from the pipes while Debbie and I stood at each end of the table ready to help. "She's not that heavy. I think she's hollow inside," Roxanne remarked as she lifted her down.

We helped carry her to the center of the room, Debbie holding her head, me the tail. It took quite a bit of doing to get her level over the floor, but we managed and she looked real good. We glued little yellow stars in her long hair and Roxanne strung some of the twinkling lights around her shiny green body and golden wings.

Roxanne wanted to take off the swimsuit top she wore so she would look more authentic. But I figured there'd be a lot of people at the party who wouldn't like it.

"Mr. Arthur added the top as a kind of compromise," I said.

"I'd like to leave it off, just for spite. For all the gossip about me. But this is a special night and I don't want to risk ruining it," Roxanne said. She turned off the basement lights and plugged in the Christmas ones. We all stood back and looked up. "She's magic," Roxanne whispered.

"The brightest parts of heaven and the deepest parts of the sea joined together," Debbie added quietly.

"Except for one thing," I said, flipping the basement lights back on. "Mermaids aren't real. And I'm not sure about angels."

Debbie took off her glasses and stared up at the ceiling. "Now she's just a blur," she said. "But I can still see the idea. I think Roxanne's right. There's a little bit of magic about her."

I hoped so because for everything to work out right, we needed all the help we could get.

"Let's get this decorating job finished," I said, feeling even more nervous about what to do about Frankenstein.

We put the paper leis Roxanne brought on as many people as we could—the disciples, Queen Elizabeth and some of the baseball players. Finally, Roxanne stacked a bunch of music tapes in the order she wanted them played near one of Elma's big stereo speakers.

"When one tape finishes, just put the next one in," Roxanne said. "I've got more slow than fast."

"You want me to do the music?" I asked.

"It won't take but a few seconds. I'll try to watch it myself, but I'll be nervous and might forget."

"Look at this place," Debbie said. "It looks like a wonderland!"

"Promise you'll dance one for me?" Roxanne said to her.

"Well, maybe. If there's anyone to ask," Debbie answered.

"From what I've been hearing at the café, lots of people are coming. It's the biggest thing since the county fair."

I looked around the room. If you believed in magic, this would have to be it. I just hoped Roxanne wouldn't be disappointed.

When we heard Debbie's aunt honking for her, Roxanne and I picked up our stuff and headed out the door, too. I had an idea about getting Frankenstein there, and I was starting to feel excited. Just a few more hours and what Roxanne'd been waiting for for so long would finally come true.

CHAPTER 21

The next morning I got up before dawn. I tiptoed to the closet and felt around behind all the shoe boxes in the corner where there was an old photo album. In the back of it, in a little zipper bag, was the money I'd been saving. I hadn't really decided what I was saving for, but it didn't matter anymore.

Suddenly, I heard a clunk behind me. It was Doris Ray's cast hitting the floor. I turned around real quick.

"What are you doing?" I said as she crawled on the floor toward me.

"Nothing," she answered.

"Get back in bed," I whispered.

"What are you doing?" she whined.

"Nothing," I said. "Looking for something."

"I'm gonna call Mama if you don't tell me what you're looking for." She had stood up and was leaning on her walking cast, which was a fluorescent pink that glowed in the dark.

"Be careful," I warned, helping her sit down on the floor. "I'm going to tell you a secret. Promise you won't tell?"

"Cross my heart and hope to die or stick a needle in my eye," she said.

"Okay. I'm getting some money that I've hidden to help with Mr. Arthur's party."

"That's all?" She sounded disappointed.

"Mama might not like it. But I need some money real bad."

"Real bad?" she asked.

I brought the money I'd found out of the closet and shined my flashlight on it. "Yeah, real bad."

"How much you got?" Doris Ray whispered.

"Looks like eight dollars and about thirty-six cents," I said. "Not much."

"Go over to my side of the closet," she told me. "Get Gilbert." Gilbert is Doris Ray's stuffed kangaroo. I'd told her she needed a girl's name, but she wouldn't have it. I handed Gilbert to her and she yanked the baby out of its pouch and felt around inside. She pulled out a wad of bills.

"Where'd you get that?" I asked.

She shrugged. "Birthdays and stuff. The tooth fairy." I counted over twenty dollars. "Take it if you need it," she said.

"I can't. I don't know when I can pay it back. Besides, what are you gonna make me do for it?"

Doris Ray grinned. "You don't have to pay me back." Her eyes were shining like Christmas.

I hugged her. "You're a good kid. Now, I'm putting you back in bed. I have to walk somewhere and you'll have to stay here."

"No," she said, stomping her good foot quiet enough so that Mama and Daddy wouldn't hear. "I wanta go. I'll ride in the wagon."

I sighed. There's times when you know you can't argue with Doris Ray. So we got dressed, took the money, and left a note for Mama in case she checked our room before we got back.

The Harrises probably live about two miles from us. It'd be hard pulling that wagon all that way, but I figured it'd all be worth it in the long run. Frankenstein just needed a little bait and I had it. When we got there, it was just after seven o'clock.

I pulled Doris Ray to the front door and we rang the bell. No one answered, so we rang again. Still no answer.

"Great," I said. "We came all this way for nothing."

"Why didn't you call first?" Doris Ray asked.

"I wanted to catch him off guard," I said. Plus, I didn't want to have to make up a lie to tell his parents if they answered the phone.

"Try again," Doris Ray said. So I rang again, three short spurts.

This time we heard someone coming. *Please don't let it be one of his parents*, I thought.

"Who is it?" came a scratchy-sounding voice. It was Frankenstein.

"It's Jesse. And my sister."

"What d'ya want?" he asked. "It's practically night."

"I need to talk to you."

"Sorry, we don't want any."

"We're not selling anything. Please open the door."

"Forget it." Frankenstein's favorite line.

Then Doris Ray started her howling. It sounded just like the dogs in *101 Dalmatians*. "What do you think you're doing?" I hissed.

In about two seconds the door swung open.

"What in the . . . ," Frankenstein said, looking all around for where the noise came from.

"Listen, Franklin, about making sketches at the party—"

"I believe I already said *no*!" he interrupted me.

"Here's twenty-eight dollars and thirty-six cents. That's more than fourteen dollars an hour if you only stay two hours. So can you come?" I spoke as fast as I could hoping he wouldn't shut the door. If it wasn't enough, I didn't know what I'd do. He had to be at the party.

"Please?" I asked.

He took the money from my hand. "You want me to draw pictures of the people there?" he said.

"Yeah, just things going on, whatever."

"You're willing to pay me this much money?"

I nodded. "You are a good artist," I forced myself to say.

"I guess," he grumbled.

"You'll be there? Promise?" My heart was beating fast.

"Okay. I'll be there." He looked at Doris Ray sitting

in the wagon. "Were you the one making all the noise out here?" He squatted down and looked her in the eyes.

Doris Ray started howling again and Frankenstein grinned at her.

"That's pretty cool," he said.

Doris Ray shrugged. "Some of that money was mine. Twenty dollars. I saved it."

Frankenstein looked at the bills in his hand. Then he shoved them in his pocket. "Well, since most of this is your money, I guess I'll have to come, won't I?"

I had never seen him act so friendly—except that he took all our money.

"We've got to go," I said, looking at my watch. "We have a lot to do before tonight. See you at the museum around seven-thirty." I turned the wagon around and started back down the driveway.

When we got home, we were in luck. No one was up yet, so I tore up the note I'd written.

"We don't have any money now," Doris Ray said.

"Nope," I said. I was feeling kind of bad about it. "I'm sorry, Doris Ray."

"It's all right," she said. "I love Mr. Arthur."

We both crawled back in bed and lay there awhile, until I could smell Daddy's coffee.

CHAPTER 22

Late that afternoon, Roxanne French-braided my hair and put some blue starlight shadow on my eyelids. "Your eyelashes are so long," she said as she brushed some mascara onto them. "Keep using this 'Grow Thick' stuff and they'll just get longer and fuller."

"Like that breast developer thing you ordered? Where'd that get me?" I teased.

"Just give them time. They don't sprout up overnight, you know," Roxanne said, stepping back to look at the whole effect of my makeup.

"You're lucky you don't need base or blush," she said.

I got tickled.

"What's the matter?" she asked.

"'They don't sprout up overnight,'" I repeated, laughing. "Like you're talking about radishes."

Roxanne was trying to sprinkle a little glitter in my hair and she burst out laughing.

"This aunt of mine named Urla called hers peaches," I choked.

"Urla? Is that a name for a human being? Urla?" Roxanne was laughing so hard she was holding her stomach. "She called her boobies *peaches*?"

"Yeah," I said. "She had six kids and she breast-fed each one. She told Mama those babies stretched her all the way to Kingdom Come."

By this time, we were both rolling on the floor, giggling. Roxanne was trying to catch her breath, and she had tears rolling down her cheeks.

Then Roxanne's voice got as soft and quiet as the wind before a storm. "Jesse, I never got to nurse a baby. When Franklin was born, I was so full of milk I was about to pop. They gave me some kind of shot to dry it up, but I remember lying in that hospital bed crying and oozing milk all over the place."

I changed the subject. "Mama and Daddy are going to Mr. Arthur's, too. I can come over and ride with you, though."

Roxanne shook her head slowly. "No, you go ahead and ride with them. I might be a little late."

"Late? Tonight? The most important night of the year?"

"You can handle it. Get things going for me."

"Are you nervous?" I asked.

"A little. But it'll be all right. Jesse?"

"Um?"

"Do you remember coming back from the hospital with Doris Ray, how you told me about William III?"

"What's that got to do with tonight?" I asked.

"Nothing, except you said you never got to tell him goodbye."

"So?"

"I was thinking. You can't ever see your brother again. Maybe that's why you needed to say goodbye. But someday, I may see Franklin again. There's always that chance."

I wasn't so sure, but I nodded anyway.

She bent down and kissed me on the forehead. "You run on home. Get Doris Ray all fixed up. And here, take her these."

She handed me the silver high heels she'd worn to the hospital, the ones Doris Ray went nuts over.

"She's only got one good foot, remember?" I said.

"Knowing Doris Ray, she'll figure out something," Roxanne said.

"Yeah, she'll be excited. Are you okay?" I asked.

"I'm fine. It's just that the night's finally here. And I thought it never would be. Thanks, Jesse. You made it happen."

"Well, not yet. Franklin—"

"Oh, he'll be there. There's a full moon tonight. Now go!" She grinned and pushed me toward the door. When I got outside on the grass, she hollered, "I'll see you under the mermaid angel!"

By the time I got home there was so much to do I didn't even think about Roxanne again until the party had already started.

CHAPTER 23

Doris Ray begged and whined and pleaded and she finally got to wear one of Roxanne's silver high heels with her Easter dress, which was made out of a stiff blue stuff that stood out like a tent and squeaked when you rubbed against it.

"How can you let her go to the party like that?" I asked Mama. She looked ridiculous, plus she could trip and break her other leg.

"There's going to be no arguments tonight. No matter what. I haven't danced with your daddy in four years, and a high-heeled shoe will not ruin my night." Mama went on to say Doris Ray had agreed to be pulled in the wagon, so she wouldn't be running around.

It struck me that Mama really looked forward to the party. I noticed, too, how pretty she looked in her pale green dress, the one she wore every year in the spring.

Her hair, which she usually pulled back with bobby pins, waved around her face and shined golden brown. Even Daddy dressed up. He wore his dress boots and the bolo tie with the longhorn clasp on it. The boys had on navy slacks and suspenders.

Everybody but me seemed excited. It's not that I didn't look all right. Mama had let me pick my own pattern and material for my Easter dress this year, and it was simple and white. I liked it. My hair still looked pretty from Roxanne's fixing it and I even had on a little lipstick. It was just that so much depended on everything going right tonight.

When we got to Mr. Arthur's, Elma was already letting people in. She was standing just inside the basement door handing out some extra leis she'd bought at the dime store. I could tell she was enjoying acting real important.

She wore a plastic grass skirt over her yellow pantsuit, and she had big white carnations stuck in her hair, one over each ear. Her lei hung around her neck with her camera.

"Come right on in," she said to us. "Welcome to *Hi-wa-ya*. Y'all feel free to mosey around and have some refreshments. There'll be dancin' pretty soon."

She tossed a lei to each of us, then pulled me over. "That Roxanne's not here yet."

"She might be a little late," I told her. I glanced around, hoping I'd see Frankenstein. "I'll get the music started."

The wheels on Doris Ray's wagon creaked as we went across the cement floor, which Mr. Arthur had painted blue a long time ago. With all the twinkling lights, it almost looked like water.

We walked past Queen Elizabeth and on into the big room where lots of people were milling around. There was Frankenstein, sitting at the table with the disciples.

"Need some help?" came a familiar voice from behind. I whirled around.

"Hello, Jesse, dear." It was Mrs. Noble and her husband. She looked real different in a shimmery silver dress. I'd never seen Mr. Noble before. He was bald except for a little tuft of hair over each ear, and his body was short and round. He laughed like Santa Claus.

"Jesse," he said, laughing as he spoke, "Shirley has told me that you're in charge of this great party." His eyes sparkled. "Did you do all this decorating or did you hire a designer?"

"I helped," I said, "along with my friend Roxanne and Debbie." I pointed toward the punch bowl where Debbie was standing filling cups.

"Wow! Wow! Wow!" Doris Ray piped up. "It's so pretty in here!"

"So are you the mistress of ceremonies tonight?" Mrs. Noble asked me, looking around and smiling at everything.

"No. That's Roxanne. She's a lot better at speaking in front of people than I am. When she gets here, she'll give the goodbye speech."

I searched the room, hoping to see her in a corner somewhere. Earlier that afternoon when she was doing my hair, I'd asked her if she'd written the speech yet.

She'd said it doesn't do any good to write down heart things.

Debbie waved and walked toward me. "Look at you!" I said. She was wearing a beautiful black dress that had super-thin straps. "Are those real diamonds?" I asked, touching the sparkling stones dangling from her ears.

"My mother's," she said, smiling. "Where's Roxanne?"

"I wish I knew." Someone walked up from behind and tapped my shoulder. I jumped.

"Wanta dance?" It was Rodney Grey, the cute guy I'd hoped was Roxanne's son.

I was about to say I guessed so when Elma butted in. She said, "I'm turning the music off, so you can be heard. I got Daddy buckled into his chair, obvious reasons. I'll put him up there next to you."

"I'm not giving the speech. Roxanne is," I said.

Elma wrinkled her nose and cleared her throat. "Well, I think just about everybody's here, and Daddy's being pretty good right now, but he's not gonna last forever. He's even keeping his party hat on." She gestured toward where he sat in a chair wearing a little pointed birthday hat and a lei.

Like a bulldozer, Elma pushed me toward the center of the room while I gave Rodney a look that said I was sorry.

"Go on," Elma whispered. I looked around again, making sure Roxanne hadn't come in. Mr. Arthur rocked back and forth in his chair singing something.

"It's too noisy," I complained to her. "Let's wait."

She stepped on top of a chair and put a silver gym

whistle in her mouth. After she'd blown it a couple of times, everything got quiet.

"Thank y'all for making it out here tonight," she started. "We'll get the dance going again in a few minutes, but first, Jesse here, who had a big part in planning this shindig for Daddy, wants to say a few words."

She climbed down from the chair and told me to get up on it so everyone could see and hear good.

I coughed. If Roxanne walked in, I'd let her take over. I waited a couple of seconds, looked at Debbie and mouthed, "Roxanne?"

She shook her head and gave me a thumbs-up sign.

I took a deep breath. "We are here tonight to honor Mr. Alexander Arthur," I said as loudly as I could, even though my voice was shaking. Any minute, it seemed, I could let it go and it would whirl around out of control, like a kite that's been let loose, and come crashing to the ground. I took another deep breath.

"Mr. Arthur means a lot to many of you. He means a lot to me." I held my hands together to keep them from trembling.

"When I was a little girl, he and Ruby gave me the job of dusting the museum. They made me feel special, and I'm sure they made you feel that way, too, when you came to visit." I saw a lot of people smile and nod.

"A good friend of mine says the only true thing in life is love. Mr. Arthur and Ruby knew how to love. I guess in a way they planted seeds of love in all our hearts. Mr. Arthur, we'll sure miss you when you're moved away." I stepped down from the chair and gave him a hug and kiss on the cheek.

The crowd clapped and cheered and all of a sudden I realized I wasn't so nervous anymore. Somebody started the music up, and I saw Debbie talking to Harold. She took his hand and pulled him out on the dance floor. He was smiling like he didn't mind at all.

Mama got Daddy on the floor, too. I watched as Daddy put his arms around her, bumping into our moons and stars with the top of his cowboy hat. They still knew how to do the two-step and they were having a good time.

Things seemed to be working out pretty well, except for the most important part. I was worried, but I figured Roxanne'd probably show up at the last minute. Thankfully, Frankenstein was still sitting between Peter and Matthew, sketching.

I sat down in the wagon with Doris Ray and waited. Rodney was already dancing with someone else and he didn't look like he'd change his mind about it anytime soon. I kept checking my watch, holding my wrist up to one of the Christmas lights so that I could see the dial.

By nine-thirty people were leaving, hugging Mr. Arthur, telling him they'd see him at Purple Paradise.

I looked at Frankenstein. He didn't look like he was going anywhere. His parents hadn't come, so I hoped maybe he'd stay for a while longer. Roxanne could still show up.

"Jesse, Jesse," Doris Ray tugged at my sleeve. "I want to go see Frankie's pictures." I guessed we might as well and pulled the wagon over there next to him.

"Let me see, Frankie," Doris Ray begged. He flipped through the pages of his spiral drawing pad and showed her a sketch of herself lounging in the wagon, one foot with her toes sticking out of a cast, the other with a glittery high heel propped on a pillow. She giggled.

"That's good, Frankie. Show me another one. Show me one of Jesse." He went back a couple of pages and showed her a picture of me chewing on a fingernail, looking worried.

"That looks just like Jesse!" Doris Ray shrieked. "And there's Mama and Daddy dancing," she said, pointing to an image in the background.

"You're a *real* artist, Frankie," she said, looking up at him like he was Superman. He stood and walked around the front of the table to the wagon. He bent down and looked right at Doris Ray.

"You think so, kid? Here, I've got something for you." He reached down into his pants pocket.

"Is it bubble gum?" Doris Ray asked.

He pulled out a wad of bills. "No, it's your money. You accidentally left it."

"We did? I thought you wouldn't—" I squeezed her shoulder a little like Mrs. Noble does.

"Ouch!" she said.

"Those pictures are really good," I told him. "Thank you. I mean it."

"It's okay," he said real soft, looking down at his feet.

Somehow with the tiny lights blinking around him, and the wax Jesus behind him, he looked almost cute. He was wearing a short-sleeved shirt, and I followed his arm from the edge of his sleeve down to his hand. His forearm was muscular and smooth, and his hand gripped his pencil with confidence.

"Where'd you learn to draw like that?" I asked.

"I don't know," he said. "My mother says I was born with talent, but . . . " He shrugged.

"You haven't seen my friend around, have you?" I asked. "The woman who came to church with me?"

"The one who escaped from the gorilla cage?"

"Pardon me?"

"The redhead with the big furry coat."

"Yes, her. She was supposed to be here." I was feeling kind of sick inside my stomach.

"Nope, no gorillas here tonight," he said, thumbing through his tablet. I pulled Doris Ray over to the punch table and poured us each a cup of pineapple juice, then sat down so that I could keep my eye on the door.

Debbie and Harold were talking, standing next to the wall near Mr. Arthur's buffalo. Discussing the quantum theory or *Moby Dick* probably.

Elma was going around patting people on the back telling them she was glad they came. She still had on her grass skirt, but she had taken off her heels and was going barefoot. Mr. Arthur had fallen asleep with his party hat sitting crooked on his head.

Mama said it was time to go, but I told her I needed to stay and help clean up. "Roxanne'll still come," I said. "She probably had to work late. I'll have her bring me home. Please?"

Mama agreed, and when just about everyone had left, except the Nobles, Debbie, Frankenstein and me, Elma announced she was going to play one more song. "In honor of the full moon," she said. "And in honor of Jesse!"

I gazed up at the mermaid angel, which was gently rocking on its wires. Then I looked over at Frankenstein. If Roxanne didn't come now, right now, she would miss her chance, maybe forever.

At that exact moment, I did the craziest thing I've ever done. I didn't even think, I just walked over to the Lord's table, straight to Frankenstein. I had to do it. For Roxanne. For me.

"Would you dance with me?" I asked.

He started to say something, but changed his mind and stood up, reaching out his hand. I never thought in a million years I'd be dancing with Franklin Harris, but it really wasn't so bad.

For one thing, up close he smelled like Daddy's aftershave, and for another thing, he held me like he was holding glass, real careful and gentle. Not at all what I expected.

We danced without saying a word and I wondered how it would have been for Roxanne to have felt his strong body and to have held the hand that looked so much like his father's.

Just before the song ended, I glanced up at one of the small basement windows where the moon was shining in. I halfway expected to see Roxanne with her face pressed up to the glass, but I just saw kind of a reflection of us, Franklin and me.

The song ended and Elma turned on all the lights. It was like one of those dreams where you suddenly realize you're in the grocery store without any clothes on. I was standing there holding Franklin's hand. I let go real quick and tried to think of something to say.

"Excuse me. I mean I'm sorry. I don't know what came over me. You probably don't even like to dance, and—"

"Shhh," he said. "It's okay," and he gave me a little smile.

"Well, I guess I better get busy cleaning this place up." Debbie and Franklin helped and so did the Nobles. Elma sat in the electric chair exhibit reading the *V* encyclopedia and barking instructions. Her daddy, who'd awakened when the music ended, had gotten out of his chair and was wandering around the room singing from a bunch of songs, the lines all strung together like mismatched beads on a necklace.

Pretty soon everything was clean and it was time to go. Mrs. Noble said she and her husband would take us home, and we all went out into the night.

After they dropped off Debbie and Franklin, they took me. I stared out the window all the way home. The moon was round and bright, and just as we turned into the trailer park, I thought I saw the mother and baby Roxanne was always talking about, but I wasn't sure. Was there a mother looking down at the baby at her breast? Or was the moon just a dead planet hanging in the sky, full of tricks like mirages on the highway?

I told the Nobles goodbye and watched them drive off, then I walked across our yard to Roxanne's. Her trailer was completely dark, and there weren't any cars out front. I went up the steps and knocked. There was no answer. I opened the screen and pressed my ear to the door and listened. I knocked again and called her name. Finally, I gave up. To tell the truth, somehow I knew before I got there that no one would be home.

CHAPTER 24

I'd figured she'd wait until summer, at least. Not just leave a note bobby-pinned to our screen door. But there it was, half blown off the door, when Mama got in from the party.

She showed it to me the next morning, first thing after I got up.

"Jessica," it said, even though Roxanne knows my name is just plain Jesse, "I left for Florida. Will send a postcard as soon as I get somewhere. Love ya, kid, Roxanne."

That was it. Nothing about she was sorry she had to go so fast, or about the party, or Franklin, or that we were best friends or anything. Just "Love ya, kid."

I ran down to her trailer just to make sure. All the blinds were pulled except for the broken one in the back over the kitchen sink. I stood on an old tire and looked in.

Most of the stuff was off the walls—the Hawaiian calendar she got free at the travel agency, the black-and-white cat clock with the tail that moved back and forth, the postcards taped on the refrigerator, everything.

When I got back home, Mama said, "Jesse, there was something else besides the note. I don't know what it's all about, but there was a big garbage bag tied up with a ribbon and it had your name on it. I put it in the hall closet."

I ran to the closet and opened the door. There was the black garbage bag Mama was talking about. A note taped on the outside said, "Jesse, please keep this. Won't need it where I'm going! P.S. Check the pockets."

I ripped the bag open. It was Roxanne's mouton coat. I scooted my hand through the velvety fur, watching it cover my fingers. Then I held it up next to me, and everything was all mixed up because I was so mad at her for leaving like that and at the same time there was this crazy hurting in my heart and it seemed like I could explode.

I put on the coat and wrapped it around me. Then I remembered the pockets. In the right one I found something hard wrapped in tissue paper. I pulled it out. It was the hand made out of plaster. Johnny's hand. A note was taped to the bottom.

"Jesse, please make sure Franklin gets this at the right time. Do not explain anything to him. Ask him to take care of it for me. Maybe someday . . . "

In the left pocket was a gift for Debbie. It looked like

an ordinary ballpoint pen, but when you turned it upside down a little picture appeared of a dolphin jumping out of a wave. Roxanne had tied on a Christmas tag that said: "I got this at the World's Fair. You can write upside down or underwater."

Mama said she was sorry Roxanne just up and left, but she wasn't surprised. Me, I didn't want to believe it was true that my very best friend was gone.

It was about a week after she left that I started wearing the coat. Most people around here don't wear long furry coats, especially in the spring. But it felt good. Sort of like having Roxanne wrapped around me, smelling like her Rain Scent perfume and raspberry soap.

At first when I wore the coat to school, no one paid attention. Except Franklin Harris.

"Did you get a job at the zoo?" he asked.

"What?"

"At the zoo," he repeated. "In the gorilla cage?"

It's a major fact. People don't change. Especially him. Which is why I hadn't given him the present Roxanne had left. The time wasn't right, not yet.

After a couple of weeks, as the days got warmer, the teachers started complaining.

Mrs. Noble kept me after class.

"Debbie tells me that your good friend moved off and that she left you that coat." She unwrapped a napkin holding her leftover cornbread from lunch and sprinkled a few crumbs outside on the window ledge for the sparrows.

"Yes ma'am," I said.

"You really miss your friend, don't you? Roxanne, was it?"

I shrugged.

"If you need a safe place for it during the school day, I have a locked closet." She gestured toward the cabinet at the back of the room.

I shook my head. I wished I could explain why I couldn't take off the coat, but I didn't even understand myself.

Mr. Butterfield in science said the coat interfered with the "educational process." He said, "If you do not remove that coat, Jesse, you may not take part in the earthworm dissection." I just put my head on my desk. I didn't feel like taking part in anything.

Debbie and I sat at lunch together, me with Roxanne's fur getting in the way of every move I made. I expected her to start nagging at me, too, but she didn't.

"Aren't you going to bug me about my coat?" I asked, trying hard not to get my sleeve in the Jell-O on my lunch tray.

"One thing my mother used to say," she said, slowly twirling her corn dog in some mustard, "some people want others to be what they need them to be."

"So what do people need me to be?" I asked.

"Normal. Average. Not the kind of person who wears a big heavy coat when it's hot. It makes people uncomfortable to see someone so different. Like me. Some people need me to look normal. It'd make them feel better. It would make *them* feel better, mind you."

"That's not right," I said, picking up a french fry. "I'm

the one who's too hot. You're the one who has to suffer all the surgeries."

"I know," she said, pushing her glasses up on her nose. "But it takes people a long time to learn to accept you if you're different. Some never do."

"How do you know all this?"

"I don't know that much," she said. "But if you need to wear the coat, and it's not hurting anyone, do it. That's what I say. Even though I don't think you asked."

"Thanks," I whispered.

"By the way, the *Icon* staff is meeting tomorrow morning. We need to get another issue out."

I said I'd be there. But later in the day, my troubles grew.

In physical education class Coach Mitchell got mad. She blew her whistle right in front of everybody, and when it got real quiet, she said, "Take off that coat, Jesse."

I shook my head.

She made me go into the hall away from the class. "Is there something you're trying to hide, Jesse? Maybe you're in trouble with a boy?" I knew what she was getting at and I thought I would die. But I told her no, it wasn't anything like that.

That night, Mrs. Ash, the school counselor, called my parents. I heard Daddy talking to her on the phone. "Yes ma'am," he was saying over and over. "Yes ma'am." Then his voice got loud and sharp, stabbing at the air like an ice pick.

"Yes ma'am, I'll make sure she takes it off. In fact, I'll make sure she leaves the thing at home. Yes ma'am."

When he hung up, his face was red. He came into the living room where I was sitting, still wearing Roxanne's coat.

I thought he was going to yell. But he didn't. He just stood there looking at me. "Jesse," he said real soft, "you can't wear that thing to school anymore. You'll just have to leave it at home or you'll have to stay home from school. One or the other." He stood there for a minute and I didn't move. Then he sighed and walked away.

The next morning I woke up a long time before anyone else. I put on Roxanne's coat and went outside. I sat down under the cottonwood tree, the one where Doris Ray had fallen.

Everything was still and quiet, especially over at Roxanne's trailer where yellow newspapers were piled around her porch.

I couldn't decide what to do. Missing school meant makeup work. I probably couldn't get permission to quit and even if I could, I'd be having to baby-sit all day. I hated to let Debbie down with the newspaper. But there was something in me that didn't want to take off that coat.

"Jesse?" It was Doris Ray. With her cast off, I hadn't even heard her come outside. "What're you doing?"

"Nothing," I said.

She moved closer. I didn't look up, and I could see the peeling red polish on her toenails.

"I'm cold," she said.

I lifted my eyes enough to see the chill bumps on her arm.

"Okay, come here," I said, opening the coat. "Get in."

I helped her sit down beside me under the tree and let her snuggle inside the coat.

"Jesse?"

"What?"

"Are you going to school today?"

"I guess," I said without thinking.

"Can I wear Roxanne's coat to play dress-up with while you're gone?"

Doris Ray's little body felt hot next to mine. The chill bumps had disappeared.

"Can I, Jesse?"

I looked down at her. She had grape jelly smeared around her lips and her hair was a tangled mess.

"Yeah, I guess so," I said.

We sat outside under the tree watching the sun come up. Then it was time to go inside. I had to get ready. The news staff would be waiting at 7:15 in Mrs. Noble's room, and we had a lot of work to do.

CHAPTER 25

"So you came out of hibernation," Franklin remarked when I walked into Mrs. Noble's room.

I gave him one of my drop-dead looks. Then I said, "Where'd you come from? I thought you quit."

"He's rejoined," Debbie said, looking up and smiling at me.

Mrs. Noble sat at her desk working at her morning crossword puzzle. "Hi, Jesse," she said without raising her eyes.

I said hi and sat down next to Harold, who was already quietly working as usual. Nobody else mentioned my coat.

Debbie was ready to talk about the next issue of the paper. "We'll want some of Franklin's pictures from Mr. Arthur's party," she said. He seemed pleased. "Maybe you can do some research on the Cherokee this summer," she added. "You could do a series of political cartoons next fall, help people see that the Native American culture needs to be respected."

I thought about Mr. Huber waving around his plastic tomahawk that day he was so angry. I smiled to myself. We'd be in for another interesting school year.

She continued. "For now, let's see if you have a picture of Mr. Arthur and maybe at least one of the dance floor."

When she mentioned the dance, I saw Franklin's ears redden. But it was okay, I felt funny, too.

"And we'll need an article," Debbie went on. "Jesse?"

I said I would.

Life was already getting back to usual, almost as if Roxanne had never left. Or even been here. Still, I felt a big part of me was missing. School came to the end of May without one word from her. Not a phone call, letter, postcard, anything.

Debbie's plan to leave to travel with her father was getting closer. So on the last day of school, I asked her a favor.

I handed her a bottle that used to hold olives. Inside was a letter, rolled up like a scroll and tied with a blue ribbon.

"When you get to the ocean," I said, "will you throw this in for me?"

"Sure," Debbie said, not even asking me to explain.

"Thanks," I told her.

It was a letter to my brother. I wrote:

Dear William III,

It's time for me to say goodbye. I just wanted you to know that in my heart I wanted you to get well. My best friend always said heart-language counts more than out-loud language.

You really were a cute kid. I used to like to rock you and sing and you'd kind of purr like a kitten. Mama let me dress you and feed you your bottle. Sometimes I pretended you were my very own little baby. I wish you could've stayed. But you couldn't and that's okay. I love you,

Jesse.

After the final bell rang and I headed down the front steps to spend another hot, boring three months at home, I heard someone call my name behind me.

It was Franklin. "You're still going to be around this summer, aren't you?" he asked.

"I'm afraid so," I answered.

"Maybe we could hang out," he said, shifting his weight from one foot to the other.

"Maybe," I said, thinking I still needed to give him the gift Roxanne had left for him.

He looked at me and as I walked away he grinned, a big toothy grin just like Roxanne's.

In late June, I finally got a postcard.

Dear Jesse,

I'm working at a truck stop in Pensacola, but my name's on the waiting list for a job on a love boat. I had to leave, Jesse. What if I couldn't let go? I'll keep in touch.

Love,
Roxanne

P.S. There's a meteor shower around August 10. Don't miss it! I plan to be on the ocean where I can see it real clear.

I stretched out in front of the fan in the living room. It'd be a long summer, but come August, Doris Ray and I'd watch that meteor shower. Maybe I'd even make some confetti out of the Sunday funnies and Doris Ray'd catch some stardust in her cup. Maybe we'd even invite Franklin. I don't know, just maybe.